STITCHED

STITCHED

Peter Taylor

ROBERT HALE · LONDON

© Peter Taylor 2008
First published in Great Britain 2008

ISBN 978-0-7090-8538-6

Robert Hale Limited
Clerkenwell House
Clerkenwell Green
London EC1R 0HT

www.halebooks.com

2 4 6 8 10 9 7 5 3 1

Typeset in 11/15.7pt Palatino
Printed and bound in Great Britain by
Biddles Limited, King's Lynn

For: my father Peter Henry Taylor
Every word is always for you because you couldn't have
done more for us than you did.

And: his wife Christina MacNiven Taylor
A wonderful, conscientious wife and mother
Only those closest to you know with what courage
you have faced life.

Chapter 1

Ali Hussein lowered his weary body into the chair, focused his eyes on the white tablecloth; his heart was beating in his chest as though it wanted to escape its confines and fly away for ever. No matter how much he had steeled himself against this moment, lived his life in half-expectation that it would come, his senses still reeled from its impact.

He forced himself to raise his eyes and stare at the man standing in front of him, the bearer of bad tidings. The policeman was dressed in a dark suit, his dark hair slicked back, his white shirt as pristine as the white tablecloth: no stains. He wished his daughter's life could have been as stainless, as pure as that, instead of the tragic mess it had become, bringing shame to herself and her family.

He heard his voice but it seemed not to belong to him, its tone was a mixture of the anger, disbelief and the shame which was bubbling in the cauldron of his grieving soul.

'That's correct, sir.'

'With a needle in her arm?'

The policeman coughed, cleared his throat. 'Yes, sir. She had injected a massive amount of heroin. I'm afraid it killed her.'

Anger rampaged through Ali's brain. 'You're sure she did this herself?'

The policeman hesitated a moment, then said, 'There have been other episodes, close things. This time....'

The man's voice, heavy with implication, drifted away into the silence. The point had been made. No need to stress it, to say it outright.

Ali's eyes gazed at the far wall of the empty restaurant. A picture of his father's home in Pakistan hung there, the humble beginning from which he – from which all his large family had worked their way to prominence, up from the bottom of the pile. And it was family loyalty that had helped them. If one fell the others picked him up. If one transgressed....

Ali wiped away a tear. His daughter had broken the bond, run away, chosen to live amongst scum, amongst people with no code of conduct. If only she had swallowed her pride before it was too late, returned home to him, asked his forgiveness. If only....

He banished those useless ponderings from his mind. He had not risen up by wasting thoughts on what could never be. His daughter had not returned and better he had killed her himself than to know the disgusting fate which had befallen her. Now, family honour demanded what he should have allowed a long time ago, revenge upon those who had cast his daughter down amongst devils. In his mind they had killed her as surely as if they had inserted that fatal needle themselves.

Charles Bridge put his feet out of the single bed on to the cold floor, leaned forward and noticed the ripple of fat around his belly. He vowed to start going to the gym. No good letting yourself go just because you'd reached forty, was it? His increased weight he put down to the prison food, not half as bad as some made out though hardly *haute cuisine*. He made a mental note to stir himself. You could get fat and fester in here if you let yourself, if you let time drift without making an effort. Then where would you be because there were plenty of nutcases here who would take advantage of your lethargy? He didn't fancy a slashing or a face dowsed in hot water, sugar in it to make healing the scar difficult. No sir!

He noticed his pad mate reclining on the bed opposite, remembered Ravinda was coming to see him.

'Go on, get out of here!' he rasped. 'I've got business to attend to.'

The thin-faced man, dressed only in a pair of shorts which did nothing for his skeletal frame, rose with a bullied man's weary air of resignation. Without so much as a glance at Bridge he ambled out of the pad.

'Bloody nonce!' Bridge said aloud to the walls of the empty cell. Truth was he didn't know whether Ralphy was a nonce. But it was always a possibility in this protected wing of the prison where paedophiles and homosexuals mixed with those who had other reasons for hiding from the normals in other wings. Being forced through circumstance to reside here amongst the dross was an anathema to Bridge. If he had his way he'd hang the lot of them, no second chances. How long could he stand it without going crazy?

A rap on the door interrupted his angry reverie. A fat Pakistani with a pockmarked face and eyes which seemed to move ceaselessly was standing on the threshold.

'It's OK, I've sent him out,' Bridge grunted. 'Get yourself in here, Ravinda.'

Ravinda slid into the cell, went to the barred window and, leaning his bulk against it, turned to face Bridge. 'You give me something please, Mr Bridge, for what I tell you?'

'Yeah, sure,' Bridge said. 'Charlie, wacky baccy, crack. I'm overflowing in here.'

The Asian hung his head, mumbled into his chest. 'You joke with me Mr Bridge.'

Bridge said, 'Tobacco will have to do you. That's if what you have is worth it.'

'OK! OK!' Ravinda said. His eyes were still flitting around everywhere, like a glutton's surveying a prospective feast, except it was fear of being a morsel himself that was propelling them.

'What I hear is that there are men who want to kill you.'

Bridge ran a hand through his dark, curly hair, blew out his cheeks, sniggered. 'I'd be grey now, sonny, if I worried about all the men from my past who might want to kill me. They talk, but how many ever act?'

'These are Pakistani men, Mr Bridge.'

Bridge frowned, pondered it. 'I've done business with your kind but there was no trouble. Never socialized with any Pakistani men that I recall.'

'You knew a girl from the Hussein family, yes?'

It took a moment for him to remember. 'Yeah, man. She lived with me for a while. Got to like the heroin a bit too much. Had to kick her out.'

'That girl is dead now and her father and her family blame you.'

Bridge shrugged. He was already living with these lowlifes because there were men after him amongst the prison population. This Hussein threat was a flea's tickle.

'They can't do much to me in here even if they amounted to anything, which I doubt.'

'They're a rich family, Mr Bridge.'

'So they're rich. So am I. What difference?'

Ravinda shuffled his feet, looked uncomfortable. 'It's a big family. They will kill you themselves if they can, or they will pay to have you killed. It is a matter of honour for them.'

'You trying to tell me they can get to me in here?'

'When money talks, Mr Bridge, its voice carries far and men like to listen.'

'That's for sure,' Bridge said, stroking his chin thoughtfully.

A silence followed, Bridge weighing the import of what he had been told while Ravinda waited for his reward. Bridge was thinking that even in a protected wing it was not safe for him. Already he had been weighing his future here. This recent news was a push in a direction towards which his thoughts had already been moving. A six-year sentence had barely begun and the threat to his life had just multiplied. In any case, it was too large a wedge of his life to hand over to Her Majesty without a fight, wasn't it? Preoccupied, he'd forgotten Ravinda was there until he coughed.

Bridge rose from the bed, opened his locker door, took out a packet of tobacco and three Mars bars and passed them to the Pakistani. 'You hear anything else you let me know. Next time I might even give you some brown.'

Smiling, Ravinda edged his way past Bridge to the door. Bridge knew the smile wasn't for him, nor a reflection of good nature; it was because he was happy with the trade-off and the prospect of maybe dribbling other pieces of information to Bridge for more reward.

When Ravinda had gone he lay down again, head on the hard pillow, cursed his luck, cursed the arms-dealer who'd failed to get rid of the gun he'd used to shoot a man in the legs. When the police had found the gun during a raid his DNA was all over it and they'd managed to tie him to the shooting. Four of his victim's family were in this prison now and the court case had given them Bridge's name, making him a marked man. Damn it all! One mistake in the distant past had caught him out when he'd thought himself untouchable, at the top of the hierarchy where others dirtied their hands for you and you sat back and watched the profits roll in.

The resentment was kicking in when his padmate reappeared at the door and, after ascertaining the visitor was gone, entered. His towel was over his shoulder and his hair, still wet from the shower, was plastered against the sides of his head so that his already prominent ears stuck out like an alien's antennae.

'Ralphy, Ralphy, however do you stick it?' Bridge said, his eyes following the skinny man.

Ralph frowned, looked bemused. 'Stick what, man?'

'What do you think, Ralphy? Look around you. Ten years, off and on, this has been your home. Don't you aspire to greater things me old son, those vistas of opportunity awaiting you without these walls?'

Ralph smirked. He got it. All those fancy words, but Bridge was just having a laugh. He knew neither of them was going anywhere for a long time. It was a bit like asking him to nip out for fish and chips, just a laugh.

'We're all the same in here, aren't we?' he said, grinning.

Bridge clenched his teeth, annoyed at Ralph's phlegmatic approach. He wasn't the same as the rest in here, wouldn't settle for pathetic acceptance of incarceration. That Ralph should include him amongst the beaten-down masses was an affront. Yet, within himself lurked the fear that time might bring him down to their level, the level to which Ralph had sunk willingly.

'You think I'm like all the other miserable sods around you, Ralphy?' Bridge said.

Ralph detected the menace in the voice but misunderstood the question. 'You ain't a nonce, Charlie. Never said you was.'

Bridge's anger flared, then dissipated. He realized the fool was trying to appease him, as though not being a nonce was some kind of distinction in here. Just showed you, didn't it, how respect could soon wane if you didn't nurture it, keep on top?

'You think I'll just sit back and do my time like a nice boy do you, Ralphy?'

Ralph sat down on his own bed, twisted the end of the towel nervously. Where was his padmate going with this? What did he want to hear now? Better be careful; he had a vile temper, Charlie Bridge, when he wasn't suited.

'That's what everybody does, Charlie. You go crazy always thinking about what it's like out there. Seen men go off it I have, just 'cos they can't settle down and accept their sentence.'

'If you can't do the time, don't do the crime, eh?' Bridge said.

Ralph nodded and smiled. They were back on the same wavelength. A bit of peace was all he asked. He lay down, picked up his *Daily Mirror* and started to read, just passing time.

Bridge watched him with contempt. No way was he going to sit back and do his time. Do the crime and everything is mine was his motto, a winner's motto, not a loser's like Ralph. It was time to act. Next visiting day he'd have words with his sister, get her on to it. She was a bright girl, Bella, running his businesses for him while he festered in here. She hadn't let her university education go to her head, could mix it with the worst of them and come out on top. She'd think of something to get him out, probably already had.

CHAPTER 2

Alex Macdonald pulled in at the kerb, turned to his ten-year-old daughter. He waited until she was facing him before he spoke.

'Did you have a good time, Ann?'

When she smiled at him he thought it made her face more beautiful. Her blond hair and blue eyes, the dimples coming alive in her cheeks, were from her mother. His dark, swarthy looks, the deep brown intensity of his eyes, were a sharp contrast. Where her deafness came from he didn't know. Watching his only daughter struggle with her handicap had frustrated him as much as her but the passage of time had helped and he had to admit she was doing very well. He was proud of her courage, her loving nature.

'I had a great time,' she signed.

'You swim like a fish,' he said.

She signed back, 'You swim like a whale … a beached whale.'

They both laughed. Then a momentary sadness assailed him as she turned away to open the car door. Breaking up with her mother had been so hard. Despite the divorce three years ago, he had never fallen out of love with Liz. Those last few years of study to complete his medical degree had put too much strain on them both. Ann had gone through difficulties at the same time. His wife had decided it would be better for all of them to separate for a while.

He followed his daughter down the garden path to the house that had once been his mother-in-law's. This was the place his wife and child had come after the separation. The mother-in-law, a good woman like her progeny, was dead now.

Ann was hugging her mother as he followed her into the living-room. Liz raised her hand in greeting, pointed to the coffee table where cups and saucers were laid out next to the coffee pot.

'Help yourself,' Liz said cheerfully. 'It's freshly made.'

He poured himself a cup, grateful once again that their rows, their struggles had never ended in that cold animosity he'd seen in so many divorced couples. Liz still treated him like her best friend. Sometimes that hurt but it had meant Ann saw him regularly, minimized the effect of the split on her.

When Ann went out of the room, he said. 'You're doing a great, job, Liz. With Ann, I mean.'

She acknowledged the compliment with a smile that turned enigmatic. 'What about you, Alex? Managing that house, are you? Not too big and remote all on your own out there?'

Alex detected the teasing note in her voice, felt himself flush. He'd inherited the rambling old farmhouse from his great-aunt a year ago. It was out on the Yorkshire moors and Liz thought it too far from civilization. He had to admit it had been lonely at first, but he had a live-in girlfriend now and that had helped. The way Liz had framed the question, that certain intonation, suggested she knew about the girlfriend and was fishing.

'You know, don't you?'

'Know what?' Liz's eyes were wide with affected innocence.

'There's a woman living with me. You know that.'

'Oh! A housekeeper, Alex. Good idea. You need one in that big house.'

Alex grimaced. She would go on teasing him until he said it outright. Best to get it over with.

'She's not a housekeeper. She's a girlfriend. Don't pretend

you didn't know. The jungle drums have been talking, haven't they, all the way from the moors to Middlesbrough?'

She grinned wickedly. 'Well, Eddie did mention something.'

Alex nodded. He'd expected as much. Eddie was an old army friend. They'd been in the same regiment and they'd both been wounded in Iraq in the first Gulf War during an ambush that still gave Alex nightmares, though nothing like the hellish trauma he'd suffered at the time. Liz had been an army nurse out there. Her solicitude had helped him and Eddie recover. When he'd recovered, he'd asked her to go on a date and things had progressed from there.

'Sometimes my old pal has a big mouth,' Alex grumbled. 'It wasn't his place to tell you.'

Liz tossed her mane of blond hair. 'He's my friend too, you know. He didn't ignore me when we split up. He could have done. Instead he's been there for me and Ann just like you have.'

Alex was silent a moment. All said and done, Eddie was his best friend and what Liz said was true. His loyalty to all of them, forged originally in the hell-hole of war and the ensuing mental trauma, was hardly in doubt.

In a lighter voice Alex said. 'I'll tell him he's turning into an old woman when I see him.'

'Well, then?' Liz said.

'Well then, what?'

'You know. What's she like, this lady of the manor?'

'Come on,' Alex groaned, 'we've been divorced a while now. You don't really want to know.'

'Of course I do,' she said with mock indignation. 'How long have you known her?'

Alex knew his ex-wife. She wasn't going to let it go. Better to get it over with. He'd have to tell her sometime.

He looked out of the window and muttered. 'About seven weeks.'

When his eyes returned to her, she was frowning. 'A whole seven weeks. Phew! You always were a slow worker, Alex.'

He shook his head in patient reproof, sighed. 'She lost her job not long after we met and she was having difficulty with the rent. I suggested she move in with me – temporarily. OK?'

Liz pursed her lips. 'How convenient for her! How kind of you!'

The obvious sarcasm took him by surprise. This wasn't like Liz. After three years apart he didn't think she'd be too bothered about his domestic arrangements.

'Come on Liz,' he said. 'I expected you to be pleased for me. You and I—'

Seeing Liz's eyebrows knit together, he took it as a sign not to continue down that road. As the silence between them deepened he found himself wishing it had never come to this. If only it was possible to turn back the clock. Once again, he had to remind himself that it was his fault they were apart. His ambition to make something of himself, though the motivation had been to make life better for all of them, had become obsessive. Their parting had been a heavy price to pay for his success and deep down he knew it hadn't been worth it.

'All I'm bothered about,' Liz said, an irritating edge to her voice, 'is that the father of my child doesn't make a fool of himself.'

Alex's anger flared. Did she think he was a child who couldn't handle his own life? Words came uninhibited into his mouth.

'Maybe you could have stopped it ever reaching this point,' he snapped.

A mystified look froze on her face and her body stiffened as though rigor mortis was setting in. Her reaction and the fact that he had surprised himself with his outburst prevented him saying more.

The silence stretched unbearably. When it grew to embarrassing proportions Alex broke it. 'Forget it, Liz. Just forget it and leave me be.'

Recovering her composure, she didn't let it go, 'What a strange remark to make. You're living with a woman and you can talk about me stopping it. Don't you care about this woman? Are you suffering a mid-life crisis or something, or are you just being shallow?'

He could detect a coolness in her voice that made it difficult to find any emotion that could be under the surface. She was right of course. His words were inappropriate and really badly timed. What was he thinking?

'Slip of the tongue,' he muttered. 'Feeling sorry I don't see more of my daughter, I suppose.'

Grimacing, she said, 'An understandable lapse, then.'

To Alex's relief Ann chose that moment to rush downstairs and enter the room. She signed to her father that she'd forgotten to tell him it was her school sports day the following week. Would he be coming to watch her race?

'Of course,' he said, facing her so she could read his lips. 'Your mother and I will come together like always, won't we, Liz?'

'Of course,' she repeated. 'Like always.'

He kissed his daughter goodbye and Liz walked him to the door. They paused at the threshold, both still a little embarrassed. When he looked at his ex-wife now he knew that his unrehearsed outburst had reflected the feelings for her he'd managed to suppress so well these past few years. But he'd done the damage to the marriage himself, would have to make the best of it. He'd never asked her to take him back, his sense of guilt weighing too heavily. He vowed today's slip of the tongue would be the last.

'How's the prison?' Liz asked. 'Captivating?'

'It's OK, especially if you're agoraphobic,' he said, laughing. 'The clientele get sick like everybody else. As you well know, it's a doctor's job to do his best for every patient no matter what they've done.'

Her eyes focused on his with concern. 'Do you never feel threatened, Alex?'

He shook his head. 'Some of them are just poor misguided creatures, others are – well – just pure evil. But those evil ones, they pass us every day on the street without our knowing. In prison at least they're controlled, so generally I see the best of their character.'

'Rather you than me,' Liz said.

'In the end, I'm a doctor. I focus on helping the sick just like you did in Iraq.'

'Well, you certainly worked to get there, Alex.'

For moment he wondered if there was an implied criticism in her last words but decided not. She had always encouraged him in his struggles to qualify, even after the split, knowing what it meant to him to make something of himself after the army career was finished.

'Couldn't have done it without you,' he called back to her as he went down the path. 'I'll never forget that.'

CHAPTER 3

On his way home Alex stopped the car and parked above the cliffs at the small North Yorkshire coastal resort of Saltburn. He found a bench facing the sea and tried to relax as the breeze played against his cheeks. Out on the horizon a small boat hardly seemed to move, while below waves advanced and retreated in a gentle but implacable rhythm. He watched families strolling on the beach way below, children paddling in the sea. Memories returned, of himself and his parents on that very beach so long ago when life had seemed less complicated.

Without warning, as though from another dimension, a jet plane roared overhead, the noise a giant's snarl declaring antipathy to the peaceful scene and his attempts at relaxation. He closed his eyes, endeavoured to shut the noise out but it swept him up, transported him back for a moment, away from the present and the peaceful sands of Saltburn to the deserts of Iraq and the Gulf War.

As quickly as it had come the plane was gone. Alex forced his mind to banish nightmarish memories, opened his eyes and focused on the vastness of the sea. Thank God he'd survived that other life as a soldier. His wounds had been severe enough to invalid him out of the army. Liz had not only been his nurse; she'd been his inspiration. She and the doctors who'd worked on his body and tortured mind had given him a glimpse of a better way of living, mending lives instead of destroying.

An old sense of shame welled up inside him. That soldier had been so naïve, so self-centred. All he'd wanted in those days was adventure. The army had been a way of finding it. But the day he'd pulled his mates out of the burning Land-Rovers, their screams echoing in his head like banshees as he dodged enemy bullets until one finally put him down, had been the catalyst which had begun the change in him. The burning vehicles, funeral pyres for so many of his young comrades, the smell of charred flesh in his nostrils, the agony of those who lay at the wayside screaming for God to help them, had shaken the foundations, the certainties of his little world.

Out on the water he noticed that the small boat had made a little progress. He watched it for a while, so small and fragile out there in the blue expanse. The picture was serene but he was well aware that, like the desert, the sea could so easily turn, vent its spleen. Since that day out in Iraq he'd been too conscious of how the whole world could turn in the blink of an eye. That experience had made all the difference, had brought him to where he was now, had fostered his desire to be a healer.

When he'd been invalided out and married Liz he was determined to make something positive of himself. Right from the start of the marriage he'd pushed himself to his limits and beyond in his studies, especially when Ann had been born and he'd wanted to do it for her.

Sitting there alone, watching the families on the beach, he wondered if he'd just messed up again, if it had all been worth it. Trying to do right, you could do wrong. Liz had gone away with his child knowing he needed to be alone if he was to finish his studies, because Ann had been a handful, her silent world a prison for her emotions and frustrations, so that when she could no longer contain them there was no peace in her vicinity. Liz, realizing his nerves were in tatters, had made the sacrifice for him, no matter how much he had protested against it at the time. Then, somehow, they'd just drifted, sailed along in their own channels. After he'd qualified as a doctor he'd realized his selfishness in failing those he loved. Embarrassed, he'd let things drift and Liz, in her own routine, had said nothing.

A gust of wind swallowed his long, regretful sigh. He knew it was that deep-seated guilt that prevented him from asking Liz to try again. How could he just dismiss those intervening years apart? He felt it would be insulting to her. He'd gained a purposeful career, his motivation to benefit himself and his family, but he'd lost them in the process; his single-minded attitude was to blame.

Angry with himself for dwelling on the past, believing that that could only do him harm, he pushed himself off the bench and, with a last look at the darkening sea, walked back to the car.

It was a long drive home. He took the moors road to Whitby, turned off when he saw the sign for Danby. The road twisted and turned from there on but there was little traffic, the main occupants of the landscape being sheep, which occasionally wandered on to the road. In the evanescent light, with nature around him, birds winging their way on solitary missions, he felt his soul lift a little. The world was a mysterious, magical place and amidst the hurly-burly of human life it was easy to forget that. It was wrong to feel too sorry for yourself.

He drove into Fryup Dale, passed a few farmhouses, the isolated bastions where his neighbours lived, then saw the sign for Hope Farm, his home. The long half-mile track to the building was rough and ready. He negotiated it with care, then drove on to the gravel car park at the front of the house and parked next to Gloria's Toyota. For a moment he studied the six-roomed stone building and the old barn a little way off from the house, which he had yet to find a use for. Though the barn was run down the house was a sturdy habitat which had stood up to severe Yorkshire winters for a century and more. He was a lucky man to have such a place, in spite of what Liz had said about its solitary location.

He went through the back door into the kitchen. Gloria was seated at the table, a woman's fashion magazine in front of her. She looked up, tossed back her mane of red hair and smiled at him. As usual, her appearance was immaculate. With her well-pressed white blouse, creased trousers, expertly manicured nails and carefully applied make-up, she looked as though she'd just stepped out of the pages of a fashion magazine herself. He had to admit that her image was incongruous in the rustic kitchen. But this was not a working farm and Gloria was far from being a farmer's wife.

'Good day?' he asked.

'Been to see an old friend,' she replied.

He thought of Eddie. 'Old friends are the best.'

Gloria examined one of her nails. 'Useful too,' she said. 'In my position you've got to keep up contacts.'

'Any luck?'

She flipped a page of the magazine. 'She's offered to take me out with her – unpaid, of course. There's a vacancy coming up in her company sales department. If my face is known....'

Alex took off his coat, started to make himself a sandwich. 'Always best to have an edge,' he said cutting into a loaf.

Not long after they'd met Gloria had lost her job, was talking of going anywhere to gain employment because she couldn't keep up the rent on her flat. She'd accepted his offer of accommodation gratefully. It had worked out quite well but the truth was he'd hardly seen her. She always seemed to be going somewhere. He supposed she'd had things to sort out and eventually it would all settle down.

'You allowing me to stay here has been a godsend,' she said, interrupting his thoughts.

He grinned. 'Ulterior motive, Gloria. Didn't want you running away as soon as I'd met you. Bad for my ego.'

She averted her eyes coyly. 'You certainly didn't know me that well, Alex. Hope I haven't been a disappointment. Could have been one of those girlfriends from hell for all you knew, messed up your life!'

Alex cocked his head, pulled a grotesque face, 'And I could have been a mad doctor conducting inhuman experiments in a lonely house.'

She laughed at his antics, then went back to her reading while he put the kettle on. For all his joviality, her remarks had struck a cord, reminded him of Liz's cynicism about the speed with which he had allowed her into his home. Strangely, he didn't know Gloria much better now than when he'd first met her. She seemed to spend so much time away, arriving back late at night. She was a little distant with him too, rarely exchanging intimacies. He put it down to the suddenness of their coming together. With time, she might overcome her reticence. He was hardly the gushing type himself.

CHAPTER 4

Charles Bridge walked amongst the other protected prisoners who were down for visits that day. Two officers shepherded them through the numerous doors, one man opening them and counting them through while the other brought up the rear and locked up again. Tedious wasn't in it.

'You could sue, Mr Richards,' Charlie declared to the officer at the back as he turned the key yet again. He was a grey-haired individual with hooded eyes that suggested permanent boredom.

'How's that, Bridge?'

'Then you could escape, invest your money and live off the interest,' Bridge continued. 'There is another life out there, you know, even for blokes like you.'

The officer yawned, fixed his bloodhound eyes on him. 'What are you prattling on about now, man?'

'Trying to help you escape this place, Mr Richards. Every time you turn that key – well – your poor wrist. Repetitive strain injury they call it. You'll suffer for it in later life. You could get compensation.'

The officer managed a smile, came straight back at him. 'You should know, Bridge. All that straining for the verbal diarrhoea you produce can't be doing you any good.'

Some of the others heard the exchange and laughed. Charlie joined in. Couldn't let them see a screw could get to him.

'My compensation,' Mr Richards continued, encouraged by the prisoners' appreciative mirth, 'is that I go home every night – repetitively.'

They arrived at yet another door and the banter ceased immediately. It opened on to a courtyard. On all sides barred windows, rising to four levels, looked down on the prisoners. Charlie's eyes drifted from window to window and he wondered about the occupants.

They walked across the yard, silent and solemn. The air around, as when a thunderstorm is brewing, seemed heavy with expectation. The fear was psychological, as though a collective force of retributive justice could seep from those surrounding edifices at any moment and descend upon them.

'The monkeys are out,' a voice filled with derision shouted from above.

In a second, howls and insults poured down on their heads from each tier of barred windows. Charlie sensed, more than scorn, their pent-up energies and frustrations seeking a target for release, that primitive need to find a creature lower than yourself in the human pecking order to rail against and revile in order to preserve your own sense of worth in this zoo for humans. He shuddered inwardly. Being classed as one of the untouchables in this place was surely as low as you could get. For a top man like him it was a come-down.

'It's Charlie Bridge,' a disembodied voice yelled from a top window, like an announcement from the heavens for the whole world to digest and wonder at.

'What's he doing with the scum?' a higher-pitched voice responded.

'Charlie's not one of them,' another voice rejoined. 'I know him.'

That third voice perked him up a little. You could walk with dirt and still keep clean. People knew him well enough, knew he was a top man on the out, a man who pulled the strings while others danced to his tune. His moment of self-regard was short-lived, however.

'Bridge, you're a dead man,' a voice suffused with venom yelled. 'Hide amongst those nonces all you like, your time is coming.'

Bridge lowered his head. As they went through the door at the far side those voices died away, as though they'd been ghost voices conjured in a dark place in the mind where conscience resided with its store of retributive nightmares. But Bridge made no such analysis, just focused on that last voice which confirmed for him that he was in danger as long as he stayed in the system.

As they marched along he wiped away the sweat beads forming on his brow. If he'd wanted confirmation that the course of action he was contemplating was the right one, he'd just received it loud and clear. The word was out on him from two families now. In this place a stranger could step up to him at any time, sink a blade into him, fulfil that prophecy he'd just heard from on high. Who could live with a threat like that over his head every day of his life?

The visiting area was a large room, austere, tables and chairs basic, the décor a dull grey. Bridge was reminded of the worst waiting area in the worst airport in the world, except there was no exotic destination to fly away to at the end of your visit, just that long trail back to the cell. After they'd undergone a body search the prisoners were allowed through. Expectant faces looked in their direction and he spotted his sister alone at one of the tables.

She was wearing a blond wig, one he had seen before. Her plain grey jumper and black trousers were hardly flamboyant. Her make-up, too liberally applied, seemed to hide her real features. She was clever, his sister, good at keeping up a false appearance so that hardly anyone, police or criminal, knew she was a player and almost as active as he was in their enterprises. The deception extended to her character. He'd seen her all sweetness and light, then, like a chameleon, switch to a hard-headed, ruthless person when she wasn't pleased.

Really, it was from her he'd learned to distance himself from the dirty stuff, so that if the police investigated him for anything his own part in the matter would need intricate unravelling, if they could get near it at all in the first place. Thank God for the vixen that was his sister. Thank God, too, she'd been with him in all those orphanages: his only real family, the only one he could really trust to look out for him.

She smiled up at him as he sat down. He jerked a thumb at one of the security officers standing near the wall, legs splayed.

'Big Brother's always watching,' he said, 'and no doubt there's a camera somewhere.'

She leaned forward and he could see just how thickly she'd laid the lipstick on, the make-up too, which was nothing like the true shade of her skin. The dark mascara emphasized the blue of her irises. Bridge knew that the painted-doll look was a travesty of her natural attractions; the woman under the paint was another person physically. Of course, that deception was what his sister wanted to achieve. Like a consummate actress, she could switch character to suit appearance.

With an amused twinkle in his eye he registered this current persona. 'You should have been on stage, Bella,' he said, remembering how he'd watched her employ her wiles and guises as a little girl when they were bounced around the orphanages and foster homes. Adapting to what they wanted you to be had been part of the game, if you wanted to gain advantages.

Bella's eyes wandered round the room. 'This place,' she said, screwing up her nose, 'smells like the pits.'

'It's not home,' he grunted. 'I won't be able to stand it much longer, Bella. I'm looking over my shoulder all the time.'

Her eyes narrowed with concern. 'You'll have to be strong, Charlie. There'll be the good life waiting when you get out.'

He shook his head, side to side. 'If you don't hurry I'll be coming out in a box.'

'Poor Charlie,' she said. 'You didn't deserve this.'

His fists balled. 'Never mind "poor Charlie". I don't need sympathy. I need action!'

'Cool it, brother,' she snapped back at him, her eyes swivelling to the watching officers. 'Don't let those bastards see you're upset.'

She leaned closer, fixed him with her eyes.

'What?'

'The good news is it's coming together,' she said, lowering her voice. 'I'll speed it all up now. Don't worry.'

Bridge breathed in, held the air, blew out again. 'Thank God! But don't be too long about it.'

'Did I ever in my life let you down?'

He smiled. 'Never! And you always said you'd find a way. Me and you against the world, sis.'

'Wasn't it ever so, Charlie? Wasn't it ever so? Just be patient a little longer, darling, and we'll have you out of here.'

CHAPTER 5

Alex was driving with the window wound all the way down. Even though he'd just had a shower, a sheen of sweat glistened on his skin as the headlights of other cars caught him in their glare. His Friday night five-a-side soccer was a weekly ritual rarely missed, the long drive into Middlesbrough worth it for the release of tension and exercise it provided. One or two of the players were friends from his youth. Unfortunately, since they all lived in different directions and Alex himself had that long drive, they didn't bother with an after-match drink except on special occasions.

Yet he always stopped for a quick one to relieve his thirst at the Gypsy, a pub on the road home. It had been one of his father's haunts near Berwick Hills, the part of the Boro' where he had been brought up. He supposed his regular visits were half nostalgia, a way of holding on to a morsel of the past. Certainly the pub had changed and nowadays he didn't know any of the clientele. When it loomed up ahead he went down the gears, signalled and drove into the car park.

He asked the barman for a pint. Sitting on a bar stool, he supped it and put it down again, resisted the temptation to swallow it in one to quench his exercise-induced thirst. He was glad the place was fairly empty and cool. A cluster of bodies around him would have been hard to bear in his overheated state. Later, it might be elbow to elbow in here but by then he'd be watching the late-night film at home with Gloria. He was thinking about her when he sensed a presence at his elbow and smelled perfume.

'Get it down you, man,' a female voice said lightheartedly at his elbow. 'Don't play with it.'

He turned sideways. The black-haired woman standing by his side couldn't have been in more than her mid-twenties. Her purse was in her hand as she waited to be served. She was attractive, Alex thought, probably could have made it in the modelling world with help, the long, lissom type like her were supposedly much in demand. Yet there was a hint of hardness in her young face too, as though the world had already used her badly and left its mark.

'A little of what you fancy does you good,' she said, head to one side, flirting with him. 'And you're so hot and bothered, mate, you really fancy that pint.'

'Like to savour it, pet,' he responded, slipping easily into the familiar Teesside vernacular. 'Besides, the wife beats me up if I have too many.'

'Poor thing,' she came back at him, pulling a face. 'Here's me thinking you had that certain air of savvy faire or whatever they call it and you turn out to be under the thumb. Where have all the real men gone?'

Before he could reply the barman interrupted and asked the girl what she wanted.

'Vodka and orange, please.'

When he'd poured her drink she asked for a packet of nuts. He went away to fetch them and she opened her purse. A few coins fell out on to the floor.

'Let me,' Alex said and bent down to retrieve them.

'Thanks,' she said, when he dropped them into her palm. 'Can't afford to chuck it away when there's so many want it off you, eh!'

After she received her change she made a point of catching Alex's eye and nodded to a table in the far corner of the room. There was a man sitting there, his back towards them. He was dressed in a black coat and his head was completely shaven so that the rolls of fat on the back of his neck stood out.

'Come over and join us if you like,' she said. 'My friend won't mind a bit.'

Alex made a pretence of considering the offer, then said. 'Nice of you to ask but I'm off in a minute.'

For a moment she looked offended but then just shrugged. He watched her go back to the table and sit down next to the fat man. They seemed an unlikely couple but, like the girl said, they probably were just friends enjoying a drink together. She'd seemed friendly enough to him. He hoped that that hint of hardness in her face wasn't a precursor of worse times ahead for her.

The place started to fill up with late-nighters, young people in for a preliminary drink before moving on to a nightclub. It was time for him to be leaving so he drained the remnants of his beer.

He'd just put his glass down on the bar and started to rise when a combination of nausea and an almost overwhelming weariness hit him. He placed both hands on the bar to support himself, hoping the feeling would pass. Had he taken too much out of himself at the five-a-side was his first thought? More likely he'd just had a bad pint.

'You all right, mate?' He heard the barman's voice but it seemed distorted, an echo squeezed down a long tube.

Alex blinked, tried to clear his vision. 'Just a bit queasy,' he heard himself say, his own voice sounding to him like an echo from distant hills.

Everything in the room started to lose focus, as though he was on a fast fairground ride that was out of control. When would it stop and let him off?

'You sure you're all right, mate?' he heard the barman repeat. Then he felt someone grip his right arm.

'We know him. We'll take him outside, get him some air.'

Vaguely, he recognized the voice as belonging to the girl he'd spoken to earlier. He wanted to tell her he'd be all right but he couldn't form the words. All that came out was gibberish, yet he knew he wasn't drunk.

As though he had no will of his own, he sensed his body manoeuvring between the tables, his arms gripped tight. When the door opened a blast of cold air hit him but it had no effect. Then he was aware he was crossing the car park in spite of his body's protests that all it wanted to do was lie down.

He heard the car door open, felt the pressure of hands thrusting him inside, hands which were careless of his welfare. It was a relief to sink into the softness of the seat and curl up like a baby. He was so drained it felt as though it was all he could ever want in the world.

The thumping noise in his head was relentless. He ran his tongue around his mouth and lips. Devoid of any moisture, they felt coarse and rough. Still only half-awake, he knew he either had the mother of all hangovers or he was ill. But where the hell was he? What had happened to him?

He raised his heavy lids a fraction. A sliver of light penetrated, pricked his eyes like needles so that he had to close them instantly. Shading his eyes with one hand, he forced himself to try again. This time he managed to open them, peep at his surroundings.

Gradually, the room took form and shape. He saw that it was dingy, sparsely furnished, the walls a depressing pea-green. The lightshade, in a misguided attempt at uniformity, was a deeper green than the walls, green like puke. He fought down the bile rising from his stomach. Then he noticed a chair next to the bed, neatly folded clothes lying across it. Could they be his clothes, he wondered?

When he lifted the sheets his body was naked. Yet, his mind still hazy, he couldn't recall undressing and going to bed in this strange room. How had he got here?

He forced himself through the mist in his memory, came to a clearing, remembered being in the Gypsy. A girl had spoken to him at the bar. He'd felt ill. He'd been helped out of the pub into the back of a car. Then the curtain of mist descended again and, hard as he tried, he couldn't recall anything.

Suddenly it struck him that he didn't even know the time. How long had he lain here? He'd have to get up, get moving. Gloria would be wondering where he was. Maybe she'd reported him missing.

He manoeuvred his legs to the side of the bed, slid them out on to the floor. Using his arms as levers, he pushed himself upright. Though he felt weak, his legs held his weight. On discovering they were indeed his clothes on the chair, he dressed himself. His wallet was still inside his jacket pocket and nothing was missing. His watch was in his trouser pocket. It was one o'clock, not too bad, he thought, until he realized he had no idea whether it was night or day.

He rushed to the window, opened the blinds. It was dark outside and on the street below cars were moving, their head-lights weaving desultory patterns on the building opposite, which seemed to be unoccupied. He figured it must be an office block so probably he was in town somewhere. God, this was surreal! What had happened to him?

Steadier on his feet, he went to the door. It opened on to a long corridor, badly lit and as tastelessly decorated as the bedroom. With all the charm of a factory conveyor belt, a threadbare carpet, an expanse of wooden floorboard on either side, stretched to the top of a stairway. Alex walked along it and descended the stairs.

At the bottom was a fair-sized hallway, in one corner a desk with a reception sign hanging over it. A thin, hatchet-faced man, black, lank hair contrasting with a pasty face which suggested too many days out of the sun, sat behind the desk. With an air of bored insouciance, he watched Alex approach.

'Help you, sir?' The man rubbed at a stain on the sleeve of his red jacket, his eyes dropping away from Alex's even as he spoke.

'How did I get here?'

The man stopped his rubbing, looked up at Alex as though he was mad.

'Sir?'

'I've just woken up in one of your rooms,' Alex said, making no attempt to hide his impatience and bewilderment, 'and I've no idea how I got there.'

The man's chin tilted in a superior gesture. His tone reflected the adopted pose.

'I'm afraid you were the worse for wear when they brought you in, sir.'

'When who brought me in?'

'A man and a woman, sir.'

Alex considered for a moment. 'A bald, fat man and a younger woman with dark hair.'

'That's it, sir, precisely.'

Possibilities spun in Alex's head but he couldn't settle on anything that made any kind of sense. That thumping noise, though muted now, was still there in his brain and a sense of bewilderment pervaded all his attempts at logic.

Hatchet-face was watching him with that patronizing air. 'They paid for your room and left a package for you, sir.'

He reached below the desk, brought out a large sealed envelope. Alex, mystified, reached out and took it.

He turned away and opened the package. Two photographs slid out into his hand. His senses reeled. The whole room seemed to close in on him trying to crush him. He forced himself to look again, half-hoping his eyes had deceived him. But there was no doubt about it. The first photograph showed him and a girl naked on the bed. It was the girl from the Gypsy. The second was a close up of himself leaning over a table snorting a line of white powder like a pig at a trough. An arm, its owner unseen, was around his shoulder like a tentacle.

Alex closed his eyes, felt shame and anger burning his cheeks. The photographs were so sordid. The girl and her fat partner must have drugged him, engineered the whole affair. He allowed himself to look at hatchet-face. The man was craning his neck to view the photographs. Alex bundled them into the envelope and stared him down.

He snapped, 'How long have I been in that room?'

Glancing a his watch, the man answered, 'You came in at ten. It's just after one now. Three hours, then, sir.'

'Do you know the pair who brought me in.'

The receptionist stared at Alex. His bored expression had gone now and he looked puzzled.

'Never seen them before in my life. They paid for your room, helped you up there, came down, told me to let you sleep it off. I thought they knew you, sir. It seemed to me they were doing a friend a favour.'

Alex said nothing and a silence developed until the receptionist, uncomfortable now, felt the need to fill it.

'Are you able to drive, sir? Or would you prefer to return to your room?'

'Where's my car?' Alex said, asking himself the question as much the receptionist. His first thought was that it must still be in the car park at the Gypsy, his second that it was probably stolen.

Hatchet-face reached under the desk, brought out a set of keys. He dangled them in front of Alex as though he'd found a trinket to please a troublesome child.

'They left your keys with me, sir. Your car is parked right outside.'

Alex took them, thinking the sooner he got out of there the better. But was he all right to drive? He remembered he'd only had one pint but he was nearly sure somebody had put something in that pint. Then, there was the photograph, showing him snorting. Those considerations were overcome by his need to get out of that grubby little hotel, distance himself from a place where someone, for some reason, had dragged him down into their gutter.

Gripping the package containing the photographs as if it were his life in his hands, with a curt nod he turned away from the receptionist. Then he headed for the door and, without a backward glance, walked from the building on to the street, where he gulped in the fresh night air as though it had the power to cleanse his soul.

He noticed his car parked at the kerb and hurried to it, pleased that he was able to walk straight, if a little lacking strength in all his limbs. The familiarity of the driver's seat was like a haven after his harrowing experience. Before he set off he looked over his shoulder, noticed that the sign over the hotel read, 'The Grand'. It struck him as a total misnomer but he knew he'd seen it before and that the hotel was in the centre of town.

His first desire was to go straight home. But what could he tell Gloria? Would she believe what had happened? Something, pride maybe because he'd been duped, made him decide it might be best not to tell her. Yet he felt he had to talk it through with somebody and he could only think of Eddie. His old friend didn't live far away and he made up his mind to go there and unburden himself.

CHAPTER 6

Eddie lived alone in Marton, one of the better parts of Middlesbrough where the famous Captain Cook had been born. Alex rang his doorbell repeatedly until a light went on in the hall.

He heard the bolt drawn back, a key turn in the lock. The door opened a fraction. Eddie peered through the gap. When he recognized Alex, he opened the door wide.

'Good God, man!' he exclaimed rubbing at his eyes, 'What brings you here this time of night. Thrown you out, has she?'

'Not that simple,' Alex said. 'Need to talk to you, man. Sorry it's so late.'

'Haway in then,' Eddie said, stepping back. 'Go in the front room while I make us a brew. You look like you need one.'

Alex entered the room. It was typical Eddie, a bachelor's room, no decorative flourishes but, as a legacy from his army days, neat and tidy. There were no pictures hanging, just photographs of their old platoon. For Alex, it was like looking at a gallery of scenes from a former life and a lump formed in his throat, remembering how many had died. He wondered how Eddie lived with those youthful faces reminding him every day; he supposed everybody was different.

Suddenly, he remembered Gloria and shouted, 'Can I use your phone, mate?'

'Help yourself,' Eddie called from the kitchen. 'Give somebody else a fright in the night why don't you?'

Gloria answered on the third ring. She sounded worried. He tried instantly to put her at ease.

'It's Alex, pet. I'm all right but—'

She interrupted before he could say more. 'Alex, what's happened. Where are you?'

He was relieved that he could only hear remonstration in her voice, no hysterics.

'I'm at Eddie's, pet.' He breathed in, lowered his voice, tried to sound subdued, conscience stricken. 'I fell asleep. Can't understand it.'

Gloria was silent for a moment. He figured she was letting him feel her displeasure, calculating the slow burn of her silence was more potent than words.

Eventually she said, 'I was going to call the police, report you missing.'

'Sorry, pet,' he repeated, putting as much humility into it as he could. He thought she was taking it well so far, no explosions.

'It's not like you, Alex. You're so – responsible,' she said. 'Is this a new side I haven't seen?'

'Fatigue, Gloria. Must have put too much into the five-a-side.'

'And your pal didn't think to wake you?'

The hardest question so far. He thought quickly. 'Eddie had too many drinks, was blotto himself.'

A moment of hesitation at her end, then, 'I'll believe your diagnosis, doctor, thousands wouldn't.'

'I'm having a coffee, then I'll drive home.'

'Drive carefully. You know those roads can be dangerous.'

'See you, then,' he mumbled, and put the phone down with a long sigh of relief. At least that was one problem out of the way; Gloria was placated. Now he'd have to deal with his other problem and that wouldn't be easy.

Eddie carried a tray through to the living room. He handed Alex a mug of tea.

'Couldn't help hearing that part where I got the blame,' he said, and tut-tutted. 'I don't know. Blackening your old mate's name. Using him as an excuse. Long time since you've had to do that. Must be serious trouble.'

Alex looked sheepish as he watched his pal lower his wide-shouldered, muscular body into the chair opposite. It struck him how little Eddie had changed. A few grey hairs apart, he was still young and fit-looking and the deep-green eyes had not lost that youthful twinkle. The jutting chin with its dark bristle, the thick curly hair, together with his build, gave him a look of solid dependability. This was a man with whom Alex had a strong bond, a bond that stretched back so that he felt he could confide in him and gain a response which, even if it might turn out to be unpalatable, he could be sure would have his best interests at its core. It cut both ways, of course. That was why he was comfortable in Eddie's company, why it wouldn't be too difficult to overcome his embarrassment and tell him what had happened.

He came straight to it. 'I think I could be in some serious trouble, Eddie.'

Eddie raised his eyebrows. 'You were obviously reluctant to tell Gloria, so, if I had to guess, I'd say woman trouble.'

'You could say that,' Alex supped his tea, fortifying himself. His eyes alighted on a photograph sitting on the mantelpiece. He and Eddie were together in uniform, ramrod straight, smart as buttons. It struck him how different he looked from the degrading picture of himself he'd seen earlier that night. Where should he start his story?

'Start right at the beginning, old son,' Eddie piped up as though he'd read his thoughts. 'I'm all ears.'

Alex leaned back, looked his friend in the eye and did just that, from the moment he'd entered the Gypsy and finishing with how he couldn't bring himself to tell Gloria what had happened because he was more than a little ashamed and, anyway, would she really believe he hadn't just willingly fallen into their trap and was wriggling now. He finished by saying he didn't like to use Eddie as his excuse but couldn't think of any other way.

Eddie listened without interrupting, put his mug on the floor, steepled his fingers against his lips and frowned thoughtfully.

'As a taxi driver,' he began. 'I hear some stories. Yours ranks up there with the best of them. Like something out of a spy story, isn't it?'

'Believe me it was no film,' Alex said. 'No fiction. Wish it was.'

'Why would they go to all that trouble? That's what we have to ask ourselves. Think! Did they give you any clue?'

Alex drew in a breath, let it go. He had given thought, however desultory, the reasons. Now he ran the events through his head once more before committing himself. Only one answer seemed viable, however he looked at it.

'The girl must have put a drug of some kind in my drink, enough to weaken and disorientate me. Then they took me to that hotel and I was out of it long enough for them to manipulate me. As you say, they went to a lot of trouble.'

'The reason, Alex?'

'Not to present me with a photograph as a souvenir of a night of debauchment, that's for sure.'

'Alex, say the word even if you don't want to.'

Alex stared at the floor. He'd been so relieved just to escape from that hotel, but at the back of his mind he'd known that that couldn't be the end of the matter, that the photographs were a message left for him. Now that his mind was clearing, what had been in the background of his thought processes was filtering to the front. Everything was telescoping to the one word that Eddie obviously thought he was avoiding. Reluctantly, he said it loud and clear.

'Blackmail!'

'The most obvious answer,' Eddie said, leaning back.

Alex closed his eyes, as though to shut out the word and its implications. When he opened them again, he said, 'I'll be hearing from them, won't I.'

Eddie nodded. 'Be prepared for that. You would think they must know a fair bit about you to go to all that trouble and they must want something for the effort.'

'Money, that's what blackmailers want. But I'm not that rich. Why pick on me?'

'They could have misjudged you.' Eddie mused. 'Or I suppose another possibility is that it was a case of mistaken identity and they took you instead of someone else.'

That last possibility gave Alex a measure of relief. Mistaken identity would mean they'd realize their error and he'd likely never hear from them again. Even if they investigated him, they'd conclude he was no moneybags and give it up.

Eddie had to spoil that comforting train of thought. 'Worst case, they threaten to send the photographs to the newspapers or your employers, maybe your family, unless you pay.'

'They could finish me as a doctor,' Alex said, biting down hard on his lip as the full implications hit home, 'and ruin my personal life.'

'That would be worst-case scenario,' Eddie said, sympathetically. 'But if it happened that way you'd have to decide whether to bring the police into it or pay up.'

'Damn them to hell,' Alex said, banging his fist on the arm of the chair. 'Why me? I'm just an ordinary Joe, not rich or famous. I'm just a doctor who wants a bit of peace.'

Eddie stroked his chin. 'Could it be you misdiagnosed a patient, wrong treatment, something like that? They're out for revenge?'

'No way,' Alex said. 'These days I'd soon know about it if I did anything wrong professionally. No, Eddie, I'll just have to wait and see, but this is a mistake, I reckon.'

'But if it isn't, and they try it on, what will you do? Will you pay?'

Alex frowned, considered, said, 'I'd have to pay if I could afford it. I've worked too hard, sacrificed too much to let this destroy my career.'

'Dangerous waters there, old son. Leeches like to suck you dry. But whatever you decide, whatever comes of this, I'm with you. We went through too much together to be beaten.'

Touched by his friend's loyalty, Alex managed a smile. He drained his cup and stood up. 'Grateful to you, Eddie. Feel better unburdening myself. I'll just have to hope it was a mistake and I don't hear from them. Better be off now, though. I've already worried Gloria enough for one night and kept you out of your pit.'

'Wouldn't it be better to tell Gloria about this? A trouble shared and all that.'

'No, I don't think so,' Alex said over his shoulder as he started for the door. 'It'll probably all go away. Best to let sleeping dogs lie.'

As he stepped out into the night air, Alex felt much better. His head was clearer and he'd half-convinced himself there was a good chance he'd not hear any more from his abductors. Eddie held the car door open for him and he climbed in.

'Good luck,' Eddie said, just before he drove off. 'Let's hope those sleeping dogs don't wake up.'

CHAPTER 7

As he ate his breakfast Alex looked out of the kitchen window across the valley. It was one of those mornings when all seemed right with the world. The sky was a cloudless blue, the trees and fields a deeper green, while the sun, lancing through the window, warmed his back making him reluctant to move. He'd already rung his work to say he'd be late, made the excuse his car wouldn't start. The extra hour he'd gained had been spent in bed. That helped him recover from the rigours of the previous night and he felt revivified.

Alex sat there at peace in his own home, last night's trauma seeming almost like a distant dream, a nightmare from which he'd awakened to relish the normality of his daily round. The peace and beauty of the dale was like a balm to his soul and he couldn't believe there would be any further developments following on from last night's entrapment.

He'd finished his breakfast, was washing up when Gloria entered the kitchen. She was dressed in a white trouser suit and was carrying a matching handbag.

Alex smiled at her. 'All you need is a pair of wings,' he joked.

As she turned towards him, the sun lit her auburn hair, burnishing it to a deeper hue. She raised her eyebrows.

'I'm no angel, Alex. Just because I went easy on you earlier don't think you're out of the doghouse quite yet.' It was said with enough lightness in her voice to make it a mild reprimand.

'Out here alone at night, you can imagine all sorts, so don't scare me again, will you?'

'It won't happen again,' he reassured her. 'Can't take late nights any more even if I wanted to.'

She gave him a quizzical look, went to the sideboard and picked up a white envelope.

'Nearly forgot,' she said, handing it to him. 'This was lying on the front doormat when I got up. It's addressed to you.'

Frowning, he took it from her and said. 'Strange, it's too early for the post.'

He had the contents half out when he felt the colour drain from his face. Gloria was on her way to the door but she saw him pushing something back inside the envelope.

'You OK?' she called out. 'You've gone as white as my suit.'

It took an effort to meet her eye, to hide his churning emotions from her. He had to force his voice through the desiccation invading his throat.

'Sure, I'm fine.'

'No bad news in that envelope?' Gloria laughed. 'Not your emergency call-up papers, old soldier.'

He felt his cheeks flush now as he tried to think of an answer, wondered whether she'd notice. His body felt as though all its vital life force was draining away. Again, as he tried to summon words, he had to fight the constriction in his throat.

'One of the local farmers returning a landscape photograph I lent him. That's all.'

As though he'd literally choked on the lie, he started to cough, had to rush to the tap and pour himself a glass of water. He swallowed it down in one gulp. Gloria observed his discomfiture with a twinkle in her eye.

'You OK?' she inquired. 'Must be strong stuff in that package to make you choke like that. Not a dirty magazine, is it? The way you surreptitiously—'

'Don't be daft,' he said rather abruptly, cutting her off. 'It's just a photo of the dale.'

'Just kidding, darling,' she said, making a face. 'No need to get your stethoscope in a twist.'

She blew him a kiss, and went out through the door. His nerves jangling, he waited until he heard her car start up and move off. Then he picked up the envelope. His hands were shaking as he opened it again. Disappointment surged inside him and he could feel its offspring, despair, lurking at its shoulder, threatening his world all over again.

No doubt about it, the photographs were exact copies of the ones left at the hotel reception last night. There was no stamp on the envelope, no postmark, just his name and address. Someone must have driven all the way out here, approached on foot to deliver it, because he'd have heard a car arriving. He looked inside the envelope, thinking there might be a note. But it was empty. Why had they done this? Why send him duplicates of photographs he'd already seen? Then it struck him. They were letting him know they knew where he lived, that they really had him on a hook. All his hopes that it had been a ghastly case of mistaken identity, that they would give up when they found that out, evaporated in an instant.

CHAPTER 8

The brighter, more optimistic mood of the early morning giving way to an ominous pessimism, he set out on the long drive to work on autopilot. His mind returned repeatedly to the sickening knowledge that his tormentors knew where he lived. What else did they know? Preoccupied with that frightening thought, he was hardly aware of the country roads, the sea views or the contrasting change to the austere industrial chimneys of Teesside.

How did they know where he lived? That question nagged at him. His address wasn't in his wallet, only his name. Last night Eddie had surmised it could be a well-planned operation and, though he tried all ways to evade that conclusion himself, he couldn't let it go and it was persisting as he approached the grey, forbidding walls of Stockton Prison.

He braked in front of the barrier, put his card in the slot, waited for the barrier to lift, then drove into the official car park. During the short walk to the main entrance he tried to compose himself, telling himself there would be a way out of the situation, that it could be made to go away even if he had to pay for his life to return to normal.

Passing through the outer door, he flashed his identity card at the officer behind the glass partition to his left and waited for him to open the sliding door. He stepped through and it closed behind him, leaving him in a sealed area waiting for the inner door to open. In that enclosed space between two worlds he felt an incongruous sense of security, as though nothing could hurt him. It only lasted until the inner door slid open and he had to step into a larger room with yet another window hatch where he collected his keys.

Armed with those keys, he worked his way through a series of doors and crossed four quadrangles where neat, colourful flowerbeds were an attempt to give the lie to the reality that this was a grey, sombre place to reside. Finally, he arrived at the medical centre.

To enter his own office he had to go through the staff office. There was only one occupant at the moment, a nurse who was looking up at the monitors watching the cells where those prisoners who were considered at risk of self-harm were kept.

'Morning, Joyce. Sorry I'm so late,' he said, forcing a cheerfulness he was far from feeling.

Joyce returned the greeting and turned to face him. Her face was a middle-aged woman's, plump, cheerful and welcoming but with something in the eyes that hinted she'd seen enough of life behind the walls of Her Majesty's Prison to temper her openness with shrewd perspicacity if need be.

Alex, afraid she could see he was off centre, broke eye contact, glanced at the monitors and said, 'Nothing moving in the jungle, then?'

'Most of the prisoners are in the exercise yard, the staff too, so it's quiet at the moment.'

'Not too quiet, I hope, like the soldiers say in the Westerns before the Indians attack and all hell breaks loose.'

Joyce smiled at his analogy. 'Well, as you well know,' she mused, 'some of our guys are in hell themselves, aren't they? and nearly all of their own making.'

Alex forced a wry grin. 'So where are we right now, Joyce, you and I?'

She thought for a moment before she answered, 'Custodians of hell, maybe? But then hell isn't a place, is it? It's more in their minds – our minds – isn't it?'

Alex nodded, thinking he'd have to be careful with his own mind. Joyce had hit an appropriate note, he hoped by accident rather than by detecting his current torment.

'And given half a chance, Joyce, they can get into our minds and manipulate us if we allow them to.'

'But we're stronger than them, aren't we? That's the difference.'

'Hope so,' he replied. 'Anyway, I'll take my reluctant mind into the office and manipulate it to catch up with all that hellish paperwork I've been avoiding.'

'See you at lunch, maybe,' she said and turned back to her own work.

Once he was in his office he shut the door, sat at his desk and tried to work, writing up medical reports, prescriptions and other administrative necessities. But he found concentration difficult, his work-rate painfully slow, like wading through a swamp carrying a heavy weight. His concerns over those damaging, obscene photographs kept slithering into his brain like the snake into the Garden of Eden, disrupting good intentions, except this place was hardly a paradise on earth.

The outside world interceded in his struggle when the telephone rang. He picked it off the cradle, composed himself and said, 'Doctor Macdonald here.'

'Here, there and everywhere, eh, Doctor Macdonald!'

Alex couldn't recognize the voice. His brow wrinkled into a frown. Who was this trying to be funny when he wasn't in the mood?

'Afraid you'll have to come to the point. I'm rather busy.' He was conscious how priggish his words made him sound.

He heard the man on the other end snort with what sounded like contempt.

'A busy, busy bee, that's you right enough, Doc. But we didn't think you'd be so high on your horse today, not today of all days.'

The implication in the words and tone simultaneously angered and alarmed Alex. He felt cold fear rising inside him, obliterating everything else, but waiting, the way a single wave, coming from nowhere, rises higher than the rest and gathers itself, poised to unleash its destructive power on whatever is in its way. His words struggled to surface through that giant surge of presentiment.

'Come to the point. What is it you want?'

'Not much, Doc. Five thousand should cover it. Cheap at the price, I'd say, to save your respectability, not to mention your job. Man like you can afford that, eh!'

Alex was silent. No need to ask for more information. He knew what this conversation was about, had subconsciously already prepared himself for it. The demand for £5,000 was much less than he'd suspected it would be and this was the moment of decision. Though he'd already decided how he was going to play it, he wasn't going to rush at it, appear to be too easy.

'You'll keep coming back,' he said. 'Bleed me dry.'

'Wrong, Doc! We're not greedy people. We've other fish to catch. We don't want the police nosing around and if we push too hard, get too greedy, that likelihood increases.'

'Why pick on me?'

'You're a professional person at the start of your career with a lot to lose. We specialize in people like you. Go too big and it gets dangerous, see? People like you, they pay up and we're gone for good. The bigger the fish the more dangerous it gets. Nothing personal here, Doc, just business.'

Alex digested his words. The rationale seemed plausible enough. At least there was no grudge involved and it was, like the man said, just business. The money involved was moderate too.

'Five thousand, you say, and I won't hear from you again?'

'What I said, Doc.'

'How would I pay?' Alex, even as he said it, felt pathetic, his voice weak, a coward's subservience.

'Cash in a simple carrier bag. Go to the car park in the nature reserve at Seal Sands, Friday at noon. Someone will relieve you of your burden and that's us done.'

'For good? No more of these calls, a month, a year from now?'

'I told you. No more trouble for you, Doc.'

Alex sighed in resignation. 'OK, I'll be there with the money but just this once. Ever try this again and I'll get the police, no matter what.'

'Fair enough, just make sure you're there Friday – and Doc.'

'What?'

'No police, right. Be a good egg and you'll stay out of the papers.'

'Agreed,' Alex said. 'This time.'

'We understand each other then. I'm your cure, see, Doc. After Friday this current malady will just seem like a bad dream and you can get on with your life, no worry.'

The line went dead and Alex stared at the phone in his hand, disbelieving that words of such import could, a moment ago, have entered his world through that tiny voice piece. Then he put the phone down and sat mulling over the conversation and his own reaction. He supposed that £5,000 wasn't too bad to save all the potential hassle, the mud which would cling if the photos were published. So many hard nights studying, too much stress on his family life, his marriage eroding, had been the price he'd paid to qualify as a doctor. After hovering near death from his wounds in the Desert War, being medically discharged with nothing to his name except trauma, he wasn't prepared to let scum ruin it for him, to bring him down to the bottom of the mountain it had taken so much toil and sacrifice to climb.

What surprised him, however, was how little aggression he'd shown towards his blackmailer. He put that down to his experiences in the Gulf. The fighter in him was buried deep now, with the corpses of all those friends he'd lost. Peace was all he'd desired. He supposed that was why he was willing to pay up to rid himself of his problem.

For the rest of that day he did his best to avoid his own staff and the prison officers, fearing they would detect his mood, the inability to concentrate properly which was the result of his unpleasant telephone conversation. In a prison you couldn't afford any carelessness because it could lead to a mistake with disastrous consequences. Any hint of it and there would be trouble.

Avoiding people became difficult in the afternoon because there were two houseblocks, Houseblock Five for drug therapy prisoners and Houseblock Three, the vulnerable prisoners, allocated clinic time. Six prisoners from Houseblock Five arrived first and presented him with no difficulties beyond the routine and, when only four men were brought in from Houseblock Three, he figured he'd get through his work without too much extra strain on his nerves, be able to maintain an outward composure.

Even on days when he was feeling good the vulnerable prisoners could make him uncomfortable, because some of them had committed horrible sex offences and it was hard to put revulsion aside if you knew the nature of their crimes. Today, only the first patient was one of those sex offenders, but his ailment was minor and the appointment short. The second and third were men who owed money and needed protection. Both had cuts and bruises from fighting, nothing drastic, so he sent them to the nurse for dressings.

The fourth man entered the room with an arrogant swagger. His prison clothes aside, Alex thought that by his demeanour you could have mistaken him for a governor rather than an inmate. He was a big man, just starting to run to fat. There was an excessive intensity in the way he stared at Alex, who'd been subjected to that kind of scrutiny before and knew it was a characteristic of prisoners who would try to dominate and browbeat you with the force of their own will if you let them.

'Can't sleep, Doc,' Charles Bridge said and sank into the chair opposite Alex as though he were there for the duration. 'Give me some knockout pills, will you?'

'Not as easy as that,' Alex told him, hiding his annoyance at the man's attitude, needing it today like he needed toothache. 'We can't just dole out pills in a prison as you well know. Going to the gym for exercise will help, as would a job on the wing if you haven't got one already. Keeping the mind occupied is vital.'

For a moment, Bridge's stare reached for a new height of intensity, then the intensity dissipated, leaving disdain in his eyes. He leaned towards Alex.

'Gotta tell you, Doc, there's swarms of Pakistanis after me, not to mention one or two of our own. Ain't that enough to keep my mind occupied? Ain't that enough to put me off going to the gym? Just give me something to help me sleep, uh?'

Alex met his gaze. 'Exaggerating a bit, aren't we?'

Bridge was silent a moment but his face was growing ever more crimson as he clearly struggled with his temper.

'You ever hear of Ali Hussein, Doc? Big restaurant owner, very rich man. Well, he's the man with the grudge and he's told his minions to get me. Would you sleep, Doc?'

Alex leaned back, studied Bridge. 'That'll be why you're on a protected wing – safe on the wing. If you feel otherwise, report it. I have to repeat that I can't give you anything except the same advice I've already given you.'

Their eyes locked. Bridge's frustration reached boiling point. Suddenly, he stood up and Alex was afraid he was going to lose it. Instead he stepped back, his face sullen, lower lip protruding.

'Some doctor you are,' he snarled. 'You're as bad as the screws. At least they didn't take no Hippocratic oath or whatever. I'm wasting my time here.'

Alex wondered if he was going to turn violent. But they both knew there were two prison officers outside the door and he didn't believe Bridge would risk it.

'Look,' Alex said, 'I've been in a bad place myself and I still have the nightmares. Stop being stubborn and take my advice. It will help.'

Bridge ignored him and lumbered to the door. As he opened it, he said, loud enough for Alex to hear but not the officers outside, 'You're a disgrace to your profession, that's what you are.'

When he was alone Alex soon dismissed the incident and the insult. In the context of that day's unfolding, it was no more than a minor irritant and fortunately it was time for him to go home.

When he'd tidied up his office he bade a cursory farewell to the medical staff. On the way out he trailed behind two officers he didn't know, caught part of their conversation.

'What do you think of that young supermodel, Johnny? The police caught her with her boyfriend in his flat high as a kite! All over the newspapers it was. What an example!'

'Drugs, eh! They never learn, do they?'

'Claims it was her first time, that it was her boyfriend's fault.'

'Well, she would, wouldn't she? Don't they all?'

'Bet they escape jail though.'

'One law for the rich....'

As he walked towards his car their conversation kept coming into Alex's mind. Driving home, he reconsidered whether he was right to comply with the blackmailers' demands. Why didn't he just go to the police, hang the consequences? But the words he'd overheard served to reinforce the decision he'd made. No matter what his excuse, people would judge and mud always stuck.

CHAPTER 9

Friday at noon and, as he'd agreed, Alex was standing in the nature reserve car park at Seal Sands holding a carrier bag full of money. The main road was close by. On either side of the road silvery expanses of water lay like mirrors on the flat green expanse of land. Lines of pylons criss-crossed the landscape and, further off, industrial chimneys belched smoke and fire. At the limits of vision, the North Sea was a grey band on the horizon.

On the nearest stretch of water two swans were swimming gracefully as though they hadn't a care in the world. Alex couldn't help but envy the birds their serene composure, knowing how fragile his own was as he waited for his black-mailers to appear. He wondered whether, beneath the surface of the water, they were paddling furiously to maintain that outward dignity? For sure, he was and had been since this ugly business started. Today, thank God, it would be all over and he could relax again.

Besides his own vehicle there was a white van and two other cars in the car park. Did one of them belong to the man he was to meet? He'd been here five minutes already. Nobody was stirring.

Two gulls took off over the water, soared over his head, surprising him with the beating of their wings and high-pitched announcements. He followed their line of flight towards the bleak, grey, industrial chimneys and the ribbon of sea, their natural home. He remembered how industry had once dominated this landscape and nature had surrendered to it. Now man was trying to help her recover. Alex wondered if he would recover from his own contamination. Or would it poison his soul?

'Strange, isn't it?'

Taken by surprise, Alex turned around. A man in a camouflage top was standing two yards from him. His white hair was long and loose and a grey beard and whiskers hid the lower part of his facial features. Like his voice a moment ago, his eyes were reflective as they gazed beyond Alex. A pair of binoculars were hanging from his neck. From all appearances he looked to Alex like a typical twitcher pursuing his hobby. Surely he wasn't the one he was here to meet?

'Beg your pardon?'

'I was remarking,' the man said, with the slightly distracted air of an eccentric, 'how strange it is to see nature back here again. They tell me even more seals are coming upstream.'

'Yes, there's no pollution now,' Alex said half-heartedly, hoping the man wouldn't prolong the conversation when he had urgent business here. Worse than that, anyone watching him might become suspicious and abort the meeting. Fortunately, the man just smiled vaguely and pointed to a hide at the water's edge.

'I'm going in there,' he said and started to move off. 'One place the wife can't find me. Different pecking order out here.'

Alex watched him go, thinking he was a harmless fellow whom he could dismiss from his thoughts. A man interested in wildlife must surely have a gentle soul. Could a hobby make you like that or was the quality already there? Certainly, whoever was going to take his money from him wouldn't possess much of a soft side, would be more a predator on human weakness than an observer of nature.

A high-pitched screech of car tyres interrupted his musing. The sound panicked a flock of birds on the water. In a synchronized ascent they rose, zigzagged a crazy pathway across the sky accompanied by their own screeches of protestation at being disturbed.

Alex whirled towards the offending car, watched as a Mercedes braked near the white van. A man got out, came straight towards him. A black anorak, hood up, hid most of him so that the only distinguishing feature was a rolling muscle-bound strut, like an overfed bulldog's. He halted a few feet away and stood legs apart.

'Is there a Doctor Macdonald in the house?' he said. Alex recognized the voice from the phone call. It was dripping with the same arrogance.

Alex stared at him, tried to see his face, but all he could make out with any clarity was a pug nose and two fleshy, obtrusive lips, which seemed ready to scream at the world at the slightest provocation. In the shadow of the hood, the eyes were just bony, Neanderthal hollows.

'That's me,' Alex said.

'Wasn't really a question,' the man grunted. 'Just amusing myself. I know it's you. You got the money in that bag, have you?'

Alex held the carrier bag towards the man. He took it and his lips formed what might just have been a smile as he reached inside his coat and brought out a well-wrapped package which he thrust at Alex.

'What's this?' Alex said.

'Open it and see.'

Trying to hide his discomfiture, conscious of the man watching like a vulture from those hidden eyes, Alex tore off the first layer. He almost had the second layer off when the man spoke again.

'It's all there, Doc. Hope you enjoy it.'

Alex took off the last bit of wrapper to reveal a fat, transparent bag containing white powder. Nonplussed, he stared at the man who had turned away and started to move off. Before Alex had time to react, he was already back in the Mercedes and starting the engine. With another screech of tyres, the Mercedes reversed right out of the car park and sped off down the main road, leaving Alex staring open-mouthed after it.

As though on cue, a cloud broke overhead. With a soft, mocking sibilance the rain came down, becoming heavier until it struck the water like a myriad darts hurled down from above. Alex felt it on his hair, his face, down the side of his neck. It drove him to his own car for shelter.

Once he was inside, he tore open the bag. Hands shaking, he tipped the contents on to his newspaper, dipped a finger in, smelled and tasted what he realized was talcum powder. What the hell was going on here? Was this some kind of practical joke? Were they trying to set him up as a fall guy in some kind of drugs deal? But how could that be? The place was virtually deserted. It made no sense at all.

He sat there trying to figure it while the lances of rain beat against the window like a besieging force. In the end, he couldn't come up with an obvious answer, just supposed it was by way of a warning that, if he decided to get funny, they could come back at him in their own duplicitous way and make him suffer all over again. It was the best he could come up with but he knew he was reaching. Just as confused as when he'd set out, he set off on the long road home hoping his trouble was over.

Gloria's car was parked next to the house. He put his own car in the garage and sat for a moment thinking it wasn't too late to confide in Gloria and share his troubles, see what she made of the latest instalment. Or should he keep quiet and hope he could get on with his life without hearing any more from his tormentors? Even as he made his way to the house and entered, he was undecided.

He found her curled up on the sofa watching television, pointing the control as she switched channels haphazardly. A cup of coffee sat on the table in front of her and it gave him a small surge of pleasure to see her looking so at home in his house. Today, particularly, he didn't want to be alone to brood on events, needed to be taken out of himself. This house had been so lonely before she'd arrived. When she saw him, though, there was no welcoming smile, only a frown.

'God, you look awful! she exclaimed. 'Pale and tired.'

A little hurt by her brusqueness, he muttered, 'Bad day at the office, I guess And there's not much fresh air in the prison. Not good for the complexion, eh?'

'Is it the prisoners or the staff getting to you?'

'Just one of those days when you wonder about people,' he said sitting down and reaching for her hand.

It was now or never, he guessed. He opened his mouth but hesitated, couldn't find a way to say it. The relationship was still in the early stages and he didn't want to ruin it, appear a fool in her eyes. When this thing had started would have been the time to tell her, not now. Even today, he had lied to her. He hadn't been to work, had called in sick in order to keep the appointment at Seal Sands.

'How did your day go, Gloria?' he asked, letting the moment go.

She sighed. 'There's still a chance of a job with my friend's company. I've just got to be patient. She's doing her best for me.'

'Well, I guess what will be, will be,' he said, yawning. 'But don't put all your eggs in one basket.'

'Oh, I won't, I won't,' he heard her say as he laid his head on her shoulder. In seconds, he was drifting off to sleep and dreaming of man in a black, hooded anorak whose eyes were hidden from the world.

CHAPTER 10

Six days passed. Alex had begun think he wasn't going to hear from them again, that they'd kept to their agreement. Each day since that meeting at Seal Sands he'd been worried, hadn't been himself. Just that morning Joyce had asked him if he was all right because she'd noticed he looked like a man carrying the world on his shoulders and was ready to drop it and kick it until it was in pieces. He'd smiled weakly, said he was glad in her imagination she saw him as Atlas and all that was wrong was that he was under the weather and it was a case of physician who can't heal himself.

Later the same day they brought the sickies from Houseblock Three to see him. Half the batch turned out to be malingerers, or broken men imagining illnesses to gain sympathy out of pure loneliness. He gave them as much patience as he could muster, then sent them on their way.

He was surprised and groaned inwardly when the last of them, Charlie Bridge, bowled in with that proprietorial air about him which grated so much. They'd parted last time on less than good terms but there was no sign of a grudge as Bridge deigned to honour him with a smile.

'Sleeping well, are we?' Alex asked, trying to weigh up what was going on behind the superficiality.

Bridge gestured magnanimously with his hands. 'Doc, what can I say? You were right and I was wrong – about exercise, I mean. Been going to the gym and I'm sleeping like next door's cat. Sleep of the just they call it, don't they? And my brain is so sharp, so productive after a good night's sleep.'

'What they say,' Alex said, a little reserved. Something in Bridge's voice wasn't hitting the right key here, as though he had a hidden agenda lurking in his devious mind and it was a source of self-satisfaction, massaging his ego.

'How are you sleeping, Doc? You don't look so good, if I may presume.'

Bridge's face was affecting a mock concern, like an over-eager gossip's pretending empathy with her victim in order to extract fresh fuel to store away for future use.

'Can't complain,' Alex said, uncomfortable with the over-the-top friendliness they both knew for what it was. How long would the gangster keep it up before coming to his point?

Bridge cocked an eyebrow. 'Why I ask, Doc, is because your welfare is of increasing importance to me. I am a professional in my own right, see, just like you.'

'Glad you're looking out for me,' Alex said, trying to hide his concern at Bridge's bizarre behaviour. 'But why? What professional service are you offering? Have I missed something?'

Like a parent indulging a child's endearing ignorance, Bridge leaned his head to one side and smiled knowingly. Alex felt like hitting him, venting all his current frustrations on that smug face.

'I don't like to see an intelligent man like you suffering, Doc. It can ruin your health, all that worry, then what good would you be to me?'

Alex felt himself colour. Bridge, with his criminal, predatory instinct, had somehow picked up that he was out of sorts and was playing on it for his own sadistic reasons; one childish tilt back at the system which contained him.

'My health is not the matter at hand, Bridge. Yours is, however.'

Bridge just pulled a face, then said, 'You think they've captured your soul, Doc?'

Alex's eyes widened. 'What the hell are you talking about? Are you hallucinating, man? Been on the drugs in your pad?'

Bridge grinned. Like a dramatic lecturer making a point to his audience, he raised an arm, pointed a finger to the sky.

'Red Indians in America. They used to believe if you took a photograph of someone you were capturing the soul. Has that happened to you, Doc? Is that why you're so pale.'

A switch turned on in Alex's head. Cold fingers plucked at his innards. Surely this man couldn't know what was troubling him. It must be a lucky hit, a random choice of metaphor coinciding with a sensitive set of circumstances, a lucky, meaningless synchronicity. He forced himself to be calm, not let this arrogant man see he had hit a spot.

'I believe you're supposed to have a bad chest this time,' he said, perfunctorily. 'So enough of the mystic meanderings about the soul and let's see if your body's functioning.'

Bridge lowered his head and his eyes fixed on Alex like an animal focusing on prey. His voice changed, was deeper, like a growl. Alex felt the malevolence in him vibrating on the air.

'I see I need to spell it out for you, Doc. Let me see, now. First, there was the unsavoury business in the hotel. Then there was the money handed over and the little powder present. My associate was wired and taped the conversation. His pal in the hide photographed the whole dirty business. They tell me he got good close ups, telling detail. So you see there's enough to cause you serious grief if the wrong people get hold of all that evidence. It might seem a little circumstantial but it would take some explaining when it's all put together.'

For days Alex had been living in anticipation that something was coming. But it had manifested itself from a totally unexpected direction, taken him by surprise and was worse than he could have imagined. As though struck by a powerful, invisible force, he took a step backwards. His breathing accelerated as the magnitude of his trouble hit home. This criminal thought he had power over him and, if he didn't give him whatever it was he wanted, losing his job might be the least of his worries; criminal charges were a possibility here. All that trouble they'd gone to was ominous, wasn't it? High stakes must surely be involved!

He lowered himself into his chair, looked up at Bridge, tried not to seem as defeated as he felt while he waited to see what came next, dreading it. The criminal was watching him, a calculating coldness in his eyes. Beneath that gaze he felt like a specimen lying helplessly under the microscope on a laboratory table, ripe for experiment.

'You get it now, Doc? We haven't much time, so listen good. You're going to help me get out of this place, see? That's what this is all about. Help me and all the evidence against you will be destroyed. It'll all go away.'

Alex tried to summon a little courage. 'No way,' he said. 'Do your worst. There's no end to a blackmail. I was a fool to go down that road the first time but no more, no more.'

Alex's voice had risen. Bridge looked towards the door, afraid the screw would hear and investigate. He lowered his own voice.

'Sometime soon I need to fake a heart attack so they have to call an ambulance. You need to confirm I need hospital urgently. That's it for you, Doc. They'd never know what you did. How could they?'

'No! I won't help scum like you escape. Get out of here.' Alex waved a hand dismissively. In his heart he was angry at his foolishness in allowing himself to be manoeuvred into this position.

'Think hard, Doc. Think of your career, how bad it's going to look.'

Bridge was hovering, a bird of prey seeking the right moment to swoop and sink its talons.

'If you won't do it for yourself alone, think of others,' he said.

'Others?' Alex questioned, puzzled, only half-aware, thinking how his life was about to disintegrate.

'Last resort, we'll hurt your family.'

Disgust contorted Alex's features. He fought the urge to attack Bridge there and then, hang the consequences, because they couldn't get much worse.

'Let me see,' Bridge continued, 'there's Liz, deaf Ann the beloved daughter, Gloria your new love. I believe she lives with you now.'

Alex's head jerked back. His eyes bulged, his fists bunched and he started to rise.

'Don't be a fool,' Bridge snapped at him. 'What good would it do? You've got to think, my man. Think hard! You're dealing with a pretty mean *hombre* here.'

Alex glowered then lowered himself back into his chair. He'd been on the verge of launching a physical attack but the magnitude of the threat this man and his associates posed for him and his family forced him to think again.

Somehow, they were into every corner of his life. He had to think about the threat to those nearest to him. Bridge was the one holding all the aces here.

Bridge, sensing victory, stepped towards the door. 'Next time I see you, I'll have details and timings.'

'Get out,' Alex said, biting hard into his bottom lip, holding himself in check with difficulty.

'Remember, everything to gain, nothing to lose,' Bridge hissed. 'We'll destroy your whole world, Doc, and my hands won't even get dirty 'cos others will do it for money.'

With a last meaningful glance at Alex, he opened the door. Then, he was gone from the room. His presence lingered on in the air, an oppressive heaviness.

In the silence and solitude Alex felt as though the room was pressing in on him, collaborating with his tormentor to squeeze his life from all sides. He placed his head in his hands. Bizarrely, images of those burned corpses in Iraq, his friends' corpses, ghosted their way into his mind, reminding him of what man could do to man, what Bridge and his ilk could do to those he loved. He'd seen enough savagery out there and it had nearly destroyed his mind. The thought of Liz, Ann and Gloria suffering for his foolishness, his capitulation to that first blackmail, was beyond his endurance. No doubt about it, he was trapped and, other than doing as they asked, he couldn't see a way out.

CHAPTER 11

That night, for the first time in a long time, Alex drank heavily. Luckily, Gloria was staying the night with the girlfriend who was trying to find her a job; apparently they had some paperwork to catch up on. By the time they'd finished, she reckoned, it would be too late for the long, moorland drive home, especially since they had had an early start and she would be tired by the evening. Alex was glad to be alone with his problem, thinking, searching for a solution, but finding it difficult to decide on one.

Several times he considered phoning the police, once even picked up the handset to do it. If it had been only his reputation and career on the line, he might just have done it, might even have been willing to serve time if the law somehow interpreted the photographs and tape the wrong way, because he had to admit they'd done a good job in incriminating him. But it wasn't just himself involved and, hard as he tried, he couldn't think of a way to extricate his dear ones from the danger Bridge and his cronies posed. His fourth glass of whisky hadn't made things any clearer but at least it helped assuage some of his pain. Around midnight, still unable to reach a clear decision and his brain exhausted, he staggered to bed and fell asleep.

Morning came with a hangover. He peeped at the bedside clock to discover he'd overslept. It was 10 a.m. already. He managed to drag himself up, dress in his shorts and singlet and force himself to go for a cross-country run, a masochistic yet, from plenty of practice in his army days, the best antidote he knew to a heavy drinking session. He threw up after a half-mile and then things improved.

After he'd managed another two miles he returned home, lay in the bath and felt a little better physically, if not mentally. At least there was the consolation that he was off for two days; he couldn't have faced work today, not with his troubles pummelling his mind ceaselessly.

He passed an hour doing simple but necessary household chores to occupy his brain. Then he noticed the date on a calendar and groaned as he remembered that today was Ann's sports day and he'd promised to meet Liz outside her school in Nunthorpe. He looked at his watch. If he put his foot down he might just make it. But God, how was he ever going to hide his state of mind from Liz? He decided he'd just have to do his best, the way he'd had to in his army days, bravado on the outside while inside you were quaking.

Hoping the four whiskies had worked their way out of his system, he set off, driving at the edge of the speed limit, never going over in case the police stopped him and added to his troubles. He was already ten minutes late when he arrived on the outskirts of Nunthorpe, a pleasant enough suburb of Middlesbrough.

He was fifteen minutes late when he arrived at the school. Pacing and looking flustered, Liz was at the gate waiting for him. As he parked his car and walked towards her half his brain was toying with the idea of telling her everything, the other half telling him it would be best not to because what good would it do? If they tried to hide, the people Bridge employed, given the evidence of their capabilities so far, were thorough enough to find them. Even if he confessed to the police himself, could they protect his family and Gloria for ever? He doubted it. No matter how bad he felt about it, that was the reality. Doing as he was told seemed the only safe option to protect those he cared about, no matter how reluctant he was to comply with Bridge's demands.

'Hurry up, man,' Liz called out when she spotted him. 'I nearly went in by myself. Would have done if Ann hadn't expected a united front from us today.'

'Sorry,' he mumbled, falling in beside her as they headed in, 'traffic jam.'

She slowed her pace momentarily and he felt her scrutinizing him. 'You OK, Alex? You sound – look – different.'

He wasn't surprised she'd noticed. She'd known him so long she was bound to pick up on the fact that he was a worried man.

'Just a bit under the weather,' he answered. 'But I didn't want to let Ann down.'

'Black mark for the bad shave, then,' she said. 'Not to mention the bags under the eyes.'

A young, florid-faced teacher was standing outside the main school building. Recognizing Liz, he guided them to the path that led to the back of the school where the sports field was situated.

When Alex saw the crowd of excited children, the proud parents and the harassed teachers, heard the noise they were making, he groaned inwardly. How was he going to endure this, today? Then he felt Liz pulling at his jacket and he followed her to a row of seats next to the running track.

The races had already started. He had to steel himself to endure what, given different circumstances, would have been a pleasant occasion. The children's cheering, the hullabaloo which accompanied each race and the strident voice of the teacher on the microphone as he tried to master the general disorder, assaulted Alex's frayed nerves. He craved peace and quiet, thinking time, but he had no chance here and his thought patterns hit crash barriers before they could gather any momentum.

'Have you got a splinter in your backside, Alex?' Liz complained, after the third race. 'I've never known you so restless. You sure you're OK?'

'Bench is a bit hard, pet,' Alex said. 'Makes a change, anyway. You often said I was a pain in your backside.'

She didn't react to his poor attempt at a joke, just turned her attention back to the races, looking for their daughter. Alex forced himself to sit still, clap enthusiastically in the right places, his mind on Bridge and his threats.

Never deal with the devil. The words of wisdom reverberated in his mind. He supposed it was a good axiom to live by but, in this case, no matter how hard he thought about it, there seemed no alternative but to accommodate the devil in the form of Charles Bridge. Yet, part of him was still tempted to rid himself of the burden, hand it over to the police, hang the consequences. Trouble was, the consequences wouldn't just be his.

'Look, there's our Ann at the starting line,' Liz chirruped. 'It must be her race next.'

Alex saw Ann standing amongst the swirl of competitors. He was struck how small and vulnerable she looked, nervous too, as she stepped up to the line. His heart went out to her, his daughter who had overcome so much, for whom he hadn't been there enough when she'd needed him. An urge to protect her, rooted in all that it meant to be human and to love unreservedly, almost overwhelmed him. Beyond any doubt in this uncertain world, doing his best for her must be his only consideration now.

The starter's flag went down and the race began. Ann and the other competitors surged forward, loose-limbed and leggy, like young colts gambolling, except that each young face was set with determination. Ann managed to lead right to the last yard when a stronger girl edged in front to break the tape a fraction ahead of her.

Alex felt a keen sense of disappointment for Ann, losing when she'd been so close to victory. Yet he realized his sympathy wasn't needed as his daughter turned to the winner and, with a broad, generous smile, embraced her affectionately. It made him proud to see that. His daughter was surely growing into a socially adjusted person, not the isolated loner he once thought she was in danger of becoming.

'Good work, Liz,' he said, fighting back a tear. 'Our Ann has become a real lady thanks to you.'

Liz glanced at him briefly. 'Partly you,' she told him. 'She always listened to you, you know, even in the bad times.'

He sighed. 'But maybe my career wasn't worth the time it consumed.' He was conscious of the melancholy in his voice.

With a rueful grin, she said, 'Cheer up, Alex. You had to find yourself, otherwise you'd have been frustrated all your days. I wouldn't have wanted that and neither would you.'

He was going to answer when he felt a tap on his shoulder. A voice that he didn't recognize spoke.

'Excuse me, Mr Macdonald.'

Alex turned, looked up. First impression: the man was fat and bald, dressed in a black suit, black shirt, white tie and white shoes, fashion gone awry, out of place here. Then Alex's blood ran cold when he realized it was the man from the Gypsy, the same one who had been at the table with the girl who had set all his current woes in motion. When he recovered from the initial surprise, he wanted to stand up and wipe away the smirk which hovered at the edges of his mouth. But he was conscious of Liz turning, that other parents were swivelling their heads and staring at the man who was dressed like a penguin.

'What is it?' He did his best to keep the distaste out of his voice but knew he hadn't succeeded when he felt Liz tense.

'Just wanted to congratulate you on your daughter's performance. That was her came second, wasn't it?'

Alex's blood started to pulse. His face coloured as though at any moment anger and physical disgust would overcome his self-control and propel him towards the man. Yet, aware what the real agenda was here, that others were watching, he managed to sit on his emotion, answer with a barely perceptible nod of his head.

The man's small eyes gleamed in triumph, then turned on to Liz. His smirk gave way to what could have passed for a smile except for the insurmountable handicap of a missing front tooth.

'Your daughter did well, didn't she, Liz? Went faster down that track than a pint down my gullet.'

Alex's eyes flitted to Liz's face. She was looking bemused, as though she should know a man who used her name with such familiarity but couldn't place him.

'I'm sorry, I don't recognize you,' she said eventually, her voice neutral.

There was a short lull in the conversation. Then the man turned back to Alex. Their eyes locked, smouldering like two boxers at a weigh-in.

'Alex and I have mutual friends, mutual interests. Haven't we, old son?'

Alex's eyes fired bullets of fury at the man. But he was in a straitjacket, no safe recourse open, the need for self-control paramount.

'Yes,' he grunted.

Again, an embarrassing silence followed. Eventually, the man filled it.

'Well, nice to see you again and to meet you, Liz.' He pointed a finger at Alex. 'Remember, old son, keep the faith. Don't go burning any bridges, if you get my drift and pardon the pun. We're always available for you in our business. Have a good day now.'

With that he waddled off. Alex stared at his back, wondering at the ease with which a man like him had entered the school grounds. Of course the reason for his presence was clear enough; Bridge was reinforcing his point that he knew about the family, could get to them anytime, anywhere.

Conscious that Liz was staring open-mouthed at the fat man's back, he prepared himself for the onslaught of questions which was surely coming.

'That,' she said, 'is a friend of yours?'

Alex's eyes narrowed. 'Acquaintance!'

'An unsavoury acquaintance, I'd say. He dresses like a gangster in a Hollywood movie, either that or he has a penguin fetish. But that does penguins a great disservice. They're fairly gentle and amusing creatures, aren't they? How do you meet his type? In the gutter?'

Alex blanched at the onslaught, said the first thing that came into his head that he felt would seem plausible.

'He did some work on my house. He's not too bad, really.'

Liz looked him straight in the eyes, her own narrowing with suspicion. He saw that she knew he was lying and, like a guilty schoolboy, looked away first. The onslaught continued thick and fast.

'How did he know our daughter? How did he know my name? What's he doing here anyway?'

He shrugged, tried to maintain his equilibrium under the bombardment, cool on the outside, he hoped, while inside he searched furiously for answers that would pass muster.

'Can't say. Maybe one of the teachers told him. Maybe he has a child here himself. Maybe I mentioned you both while he was doing my work.'

Liz's eyes sought his again, wouldn't let him escape. They were like searchlights beaming in on his thoughts, penetrating secret places.

'Are you in trouble with him, Alex? I could tell you couldn't stand to be near him. It was written all over your face, in your voice even. You could barely speak to him. Besides, you've not been yourself since you arrived here.'

Surprised at her perspicacity, he took a moment to recover, find his composure.

'No trouble, Liz. He's just one of those characters you meet and have to tolerate. Happens, doesn't it? Coincidence he's here, I guess. Maybe he spoke to me to ingratiate himself. Thinks I'll have more work for him.'

'Well, don't give him any,' Liz said vehemently. 'He gives me the creeps with that slimy way of his.'

'Agreed,' Alex said, relieved she'd swallowed his excuse. 'No problem.'

Ann chose that moment to appear. She was beaming as she stood in front of them. Alex was glad to see her, thankful for her timing.

'Ann, you did very well,' he said.

Liz touched her arm. She looked at her mother's lips. 'We're both very proud of you, Ann.'

Annie's smile grew broader. She signed, 'I'm happy to see you together today.'

Liz and Alex's eyes met for a second, dropped away. 'We'll always be together when it's got to do with you,' Alex told her. 'We're your family.'

'Always,' Liz added when her daughter turned to her.

After the last race they walked to the gate together. Alex had a moment's regret that his daughter's deafness meant her speech was distorted and, though they could understand it with a little effort, she preferred to sign. That was the legacy of other children mimicking her speech when she was younger, the embarrassment it had caused her. But at least her anger had gone and her emotions were no longer in the turmoil that had led to those awful tantrums. If there was a God, Alex was eternally grateful to him that his daughter had peace in her life and he wanted to keep it that way.

They said goodbye at the gate. Ann was going to get changed and go home on the school bus with some of her pals. Alex and Liz were left standing together.

'Feeling better,' Liz asked.

'A bit,' he answered. 'Sorry if I've been a bit of a pain.'

She looked at him with a concerned expression. 'You've always been able to talk to me about anything, Alex. I hope that still goes. I still worry about you, you know. Remember that, won't you?'

He lowered his head, wished he could tell her it all, knew he couldn't, that it wouldn't help the situation or, more crucially, keep her or Ann safe.

'Thanks, Liz,' he mumbled, genuinely grateful for her support. 'I know and I'll remember.'

They said their goodbyes. Alex went back to his car with a heavy heart, climbed in and sat staring straight ahead. The strain of keeping up an appearance of normality had affected him; his brain felt numb, his body enervated. It was as though his vital life force was being sucked out of him. Worse, his own conscience was chiding him for his own part in the sordid business. Why in the Devil's name had he succumbed to that first blackmail? And now it was too late, wasn't it? The business had gathered so much momentum it had surely gone beyond the point where he could apply the brakes with impunity. Today's events were bringing that right home and behind it all he could see Bridge smiling his satisfaction.

CHAPTER 12

He drove out of Nunthorpe on to the Guisborough Road, set his course for home. As he drove he wondered whether there could be a way to fight back, of evading the trap they had constructed for him. In the army he'd been taught to keep cool when faced with a problem, look at all the angles because there was nearly always a way out. Maybe there would be a way out of this if he could only find it.

The road ran parallel to the Cleveland Hills. Behind the hills the sun beamed down in all its glory, bathing the fields in a soft, golden light. Alex was too absorbed with his trouble to enjoy the spectacle. On the outskirts of Guisborough, still miles from home, his mobile phone rang. Irritated, but feeling he had to answer it, he pulled off the road.

A voice he couldn't place greeted him, 'That you, Doc?'

'Who is this?'

'A friend of a friend.'

Alex sighed. Was it one of Bridge's crew? If it was, he'd had a surfeit of their dissembling.

'Look! Get to the point, will you? I'm in a hurry.'

'Yes, time and tide, eh?' the voice said, a sarcastic edge in the tone which set Alex's hackles up. Deep in his brain warning bells sounded.

'I've no time for your—'

'Yes, you have, Doc. Time is what this is about. Doing time, time running out. Get my drift?'

The warning bells boomed louder, hit crescendo. What more could they possibly throw at him today? Words strangled themselves in the dryness of his throat. The voice continued.

'My friend is doing time as you know but that doesn't bother you the way it should, does it? All that bothers you is getting home to Gloria.'

'How do you—'

'She's waiting for you back at the homestead, Doc. Better hurry. Gloria's time could be running out. You'd better hurry.'

The phone cut off without giving him a chance to speak. In a panic, he started the engine and roared off. Overtaking cars where he shouldn't, taking risks he wouldn't normally take, he kept his foot down, hardly believing they would go so far as to hurt Gloria. But Bridge was a criminal. His mind wouldn't work like other minds. He would be prepared to go to any lengths for his own ends, wouldn't he?

The miles went by in a blur. At last he was home, his car spinning and churning up gravel as he braked too hard in the yard. Gloria's car was parked nearby but that was no relief. Heart pounding, he jumped out of the vehicle, ran for the back door, burst into the kitchen shouting her name.

He stopped and listened! To his straining ears the water dripping from the tap into the sink was like a drum roll announcing an execution. His heart sank when she didn't answer him. Then, as though there were spirit noises in the house, whispers from a far land, he heard faint voices. Then he got it. The television! She must be watching; that was the reason she couldn't hear him shouting. He ran out of the kitchen, slipped in the passageway, regained his balance and charged into the living room.

The television was on loud. A woman was screaming as she ran along a dark alleyway, dramatic music in the background to heighten the tension complementing his own increasing turmoil. But there was no sign of Gloria. The back of the sofa was facing him. It was empty and so were the two chairs at either side of the room. God, what had happened here? What had they done to her?

'Gloria!'

He howled her name, head lifting to the heavens in wild appeal, like a solitary wolf lost in a cold, forbidding landscape crying for its mate. In answer a white head with no face materialized over the back of the sofa. Shocked by the sudden, unearthly manifestation, he stepped back and froze.

As the shape started to rotate, with a surge of relief he realized it was no macabre spectre, only Gloria's head swathed in a towel. He inhaled, breathed out again, felt his adrenalin decelerating. She was alive. Thank God for that. She must have washed her hair, then lain down. That was all.

Her chin was resting on the back of the sofa now so that she appeared strangely disembodied. Her eyes, wide with surprise, were staring at him as though he was a crazy man.

'Why are you shouting like that? What's the panic?'

He didn't answer her straight away; first he walked to an armchair, dropped into it and sank into the cushions, wishing they could absorb him entirely and he could disappear from her sight.

'Alex?' she said when he continued to stare ahead, mentally exorcising all the horrible imaginings of the last half-hour.

He reached forward, picked up the remote control. The woman was screaming all over again. He switched her off, turned to Gloria. She was stretched out on the sofa, her dressing-gown pulled around her.

'I couldn't find you in the house. I was worried something had happened.'

She gave him a quizzical, sideways glance. 'It nearly did

when you shouted my name like that. I nearly had a heart attack. But, as you can see, I am perfectly OK.'

'Sorry,' he mumbled.

'It's OK.'

A moment's silence. Then he just had to ask. 'There's been no visitor, no stranger here?'

Again the sideways look. He knew she was thinking his behaviour was strange.

'No visitor. No stranger. What is this, Alex? Who were you expecting?'

He ignored her questions. 'Nothing unusual happened?'

'For God's sake, no!' She shook her head in a gesture of disbelief. 'Are you paranoid all of a sudden or do you think I've an old boyfriend stalking me? Is that it?'

He hung his head, didn't answer. She must be thinking him a nervous idiot or a control freak but he didn't want to explain himself, not yet.

An uncomfortable atmosphere developed in the room, emanating from his failure to speak. At last, with a shrug of her shoulders, as though dismissing him, she reached for the remote control and switched on the television again. They both stared at the screen, Alex feeling uncomfortable but grateful that the noise filled the void between them.

A minute passed and she suddenly said, 'Actually, there was a phone call. Some guy from a company – Bridge Insurance Limited I think he called it. He said to tell you they'd been working hard on your portfolio and your long-term interests could be safeguarded. Make sense?'

His heart sinking again, Alex nodded. 'Yes. Thanks, Gloria.'

He leaned back, tried to look relaxed. The analogy to an insurance company was apt as a final flourish to recent events, not least because Bridge must have had plenty of people working in his interests. They'd done a job for him, turning Alex's day into another series of nightmares. Apparently they were so far into his life they even had his phone numbers. It was as though on all sides invisible forces were watching, waiting for the word to unleash themselves and destroy his life.

'I'm going out tonight,' Gloria said without any warmth, 'Meeting my girlfriends. You'll be OK, will you?'

Another time he might have complained that he really wasn't seeing much of her. Right at the moment, however, he was pleased because he wasn't in the mood for anyone's company and being alone suited him.

'Sure,' he said. 'I'm fine. It's important you keep in touch with your friends. Don't want you turning into a recluse living out here.'

He rose, went to the drinks cabinet, poured himself a whisky, took a long swallow and, feeling the need to excuse his earlier behaviour, decided he'd better say something.

'Gloria, look, I'm sorry. I'm not a control freak or anything. It's just … bit of pressure at work. My nerves … probably a bit frayed.'

She turned towards him, gave him a sweet smile. 'Things will get better,' she said. 'I'll be more of a companion. That will help. Right now I have to try and clinch this job and keep all my contacts. Bit of a strain for me too, you know.'

'Of course it is.' He took another sup of whisky. 'We probably both need a bit of time.'

As soon as he said the word 'time', that last call to his mobile phone reverberated in his brain. Time and tide wait for no man, the sinister voice had said. Gloria really had no idea just how much pressure he was under. Bridge had his life in a stranglehold, leaving him in no doubt that, if he didn't co-operate, not only would he destroy his career but somewhere, somehow, he'd retaliate against those nearest to him. The threat to Gloria here in his own home, the phone call from the fictitious company, had been a part of it all. Today had been all about cranking up the pressure, letting him know he was cornered.

CHAPTER 13

Next day, at work, Senior Officer Webster from Houseblock Three rang to inform Alex that Charlie Bridge had complained of chest pains. They couldn't tell if he was shamming so the prisoner was already on his way to see him, accompanied by an escorting officer. Webster hoped that was OK with him.

Alex, his heart thumping, said, 'Of course. You can't take chances. I'll be ready for him.'

He put the phone down and drew in a deep breath. This was it, the moment he'd known would come and was dreading. He only hoped he could keep his composure when he faced the man who was eating away at his life.

Minutes later an officer knocked on his office door, ushered Bridge inside and watched with an air of scepticism as the criminal shuffled across the floor and lowered himself into the chair opposite Alex's. The officer raised his eyebrows in Alex's direction, a gesture which conveyed that he thought Bridge was at it.

'I'll wait outside for him,' he said. 'But don't expect me to give mouth-to-mouth if he turns blue.'

Bridge glared at him. 'Just remember you're a public servant. That makes you my servant. That's why I pay taxes.'

Before he closed the door the officer said, 'For a man with chest pains he's got a lot to say, eh, Doctor?'

As soon as the custodian was gone Bridge straightened in his chair and winked.

'Who says the National Health Service is slow, Alex?' He smiled slyly. 'Got me here quick enough, didn't he?'

The man's whole demeanour, the familiar use of his name, grated on Alex's nerves. But as the last few days had clearly demonstrated, Bridge had a hold over him and knew it, was enjoying the sense of power it gave him. Alex, controlling a powerful desire to punch him and not stop until he wiped away the cocky smile, met the convict's insolence with silence and waited for him to speak.

The smile slid away. Bridge became serious. His eyes fixed on Alex's, bored into him, challenging him with the secrets they both now shared. It was as though a devil was behind those eyes, probing the inner recesses of Alex's soul, illuminating every corner so he couldn't hide his secrets or his shame.

'Get on with it,' Alex muttered, giving way.

Bridge leaned back, folded his arms. Alex felt himself teetering on the edge of a precipice, one step away from launching himself into an abyss from which there could be no return. Yet, instinct told him it would be better if he threw himself into the depths rather than allowing his family to suffer at the hands of this man.

'By now Alex, you'll know I'm a big cheese out there. People work hard for me. When we had our last conversation you showed reluctance to help me. That annoyed me. Now that you know just what I can do, the range of my ... influence, I hope you've changed your mind and will come on board.'

'You've left me no choice, you bastard.' Alex said, hating himself. 'Spit it out. What have I to do to get my family free of you and your kind?'

'What I told you before,' Bridge said. 'Just a little thing, not much, really, to have me out of your life.'

'Be exact. Make it clear.'

Bridge rubbed the bristle on his chin. 'Well then, in two days' time I'll have a proper heart attack. You'll be called to the block and you'll confirm it's my heart and tell them I need an ambulance – correction, you'll insist on an ambulance.'

Alex listened carefully, trying to weigh how much harm, apart from letting Bridge loose on society, it could do if he complied.

'And that's it?' he said, eventually. 'My part over and done, no last minute surprises and my family free for good from you and your kind?'

Bridge grinned. 'That's it, Doc. Of course, I'll never reach hospital. Something will happen to prevent it, but that won't be your concern.'

'And that something could involve violence?'

Bridge shrugged. 'Doubt it, Doc. My people will want to avoid violence. Too much heat afterwards if anyone gets hurt.'

Alex fell silent. Bridge was making it sound straightforward and he supposed a well-planned escape could be achieved without anyone being damaged. The trouble was, as he knew from his army career, no matter how carefully you planned, there was always the unpredictable to make a mockery of your calculations. But his family were at the forefront of his own considerations and he didn't think he had a choice.

'Afterwards,' he said sullenly, glaring at his enemy like a caged animal when it is forced to accept the inevitability that its struggle for freedom is over but still rages with frustration inside. 'Afterwards you'll leave me and mine alone?'

Bridge sniffed. 'What possible use could I have for you when it's done?'

'Then understand this,' Alex growled. 'If anything ever happens to my family, I'll hunt you down. I'll dedicate my life to it.'

'I'll take that as a "yes" then,' Bridge stated, letting his eyes roam the room.

Alex leaned back. 'I'll come to the Block when I'm called and you'll have your ambulance.'

'That's us done. Until Thursday then.' Bridge said rising to his feet. 'Don't let me down. You know what's at stake.'

Alex watched him walk to the door, then called out, 'When you're back on the Block tell them it was only a bad case of indigestion.'

'Sure Doc, good idea. Cover our tracks, eh!' Bridge winked conspiratorially. 'Guess we all have to chew on something unpalatable at sometime in our lives.'

Bridge opened the door and stepped out. The escorting officer popped his head in, raised a cynical eyebrow.

'Skiving was he, Doctor? Wasting our time? One of his little games?'

'Indigestion,' Alex told him, his first lie. 'The symptoms can be deceiving.'

The officer jerked his thumb. 'Like our pal there, you mean? Ask me, he just fancied a walk to mess us about.'

When he'd closed the door Alex stared at the ceiling. He felt isolated and depressed by the knowledge that he'd just crossed the line dividing him from the criminals to whom he was supposed to minister with integrity. He felt as low as he'd ever been, lower than when he'd lain wounded in Iraq and in the throes of the mental trauma that had followed, lower than when he'd separated from his wife and daughter. Everything he had ever worked for, not least his respectability, was being eroded. He closed his eyes, tried to banish the depression but found no respite as the ghosts of young friends who had died in Iraq paraded themselves across his mind with accusatory stares and confused expressions, as though they couldn't understand why they were dead and he was alive to betray them and their youthful promise.

CHAPTER 14

Thursday morning came too quickly. Alex wondered how he'd got through the preceding days. One lucky break was that Gloria was on a course in York for a few days; he considered it one piece of luck amongst the avalanche of misfortune that had befallen him. He'd been so morose, so brooding that she was bound to have challenged him and he'd have had to lie to her. As a crutch to help him through he'd turned to whisky again, drunk it copiously to blunt his overworked nervous system.

At work, he clung to his office, shutting himself off from other staff, pretending he was overwhelmed with paperwork. His eyes constantly drifted to the phone on his desk as though it held a fatal fascination. Half his mind hoped it would never ring, while the other half wanted it to because the sooner the business started the sooner it would be over and done with. When it did ring it startled him so much that he recoiled and, for a moment, was paralysed, couldn't lift his hand to pick it up. Could this be the call that was going to change how he regarded himself for ever? Tentatively, he reached out, allowed his hand to hover while he composed himself.

With an effort of will, he eventually picked it up. 'Doctor Macdonald here.'

'SO Webster, Block 3.' Alex had already recognized the voice, knew this was it. 'You'll have to come down. Charlie Bridge is throwing a fit or something. He doesn't look good. We don't know what to do.'

Alex felt his throat go dry, the way it had in Iraq before a fire-fight. He felt a fraud and it hadn't begun yet. He swallowed hard.

'I'll be right there.'

He grabbed his bag and hurried out of the office, let himself out of the medical centre on to a corridor and made his way to Houseblock Three. His turmoil was such that the officers he passed on his way barely registered as people, were like a phantasmagoria from another dimension, nothing to do with him. When he arrived at the block, he let himself in and made his way to the room set aside for staff. The tall officer who had accompanied Bridge to the medical centre two days earlier was alone in the room. He looked up as Alex entered.

'Apparently Bridge needs to be seen,' Alex said, avoiding eye contact.

The officer stood. 'I've been told to take you to his cell,' he stated, as though it was a chore.

Alex followed him out, then down some stairs to the cells. It was a descent into a world of concrete and bars, nothing natural, and no window to alleviate the stark bleakness of the place. There was that unique prison smell too, that seemed to lurk in an ill-defined olfactory no man's land somewhere between urine and cabbage.

The rhythm of their feet against the stone floor was the only sound because most of the prisoners were either in their cells or at work. Occasionally, hearing the hurried footsteps, one of those who remained would pop his head out of a cell door to see what was going on because in this cloistered world any hint of something unusual happening was a welcome breach in the monotony and almost the equivalent of a world event.

The door to Bridge's cell was wide open. One officer was

standing at the bottom of the bed while SO Webster, his face as grave as a postulant's at prayer was kneeling at its head. Bridge was flat out on the bed, his hands on his chest, body rolling side to side while his wide fish eyes stared at the ceiling. Moans issued from his open mouth while his tongue lolled like a useless appendage. A fish out of water would have looked more comfortable.

Relieved to see the doctor and pass on responsibility, Webster got to his feet, moved aside and pointed at the prisoner.

'He's all yours.'

Alex kneeled to take his place, putting his bag on the floor. Watching Bridge's performance, he had to admit it was a convincing one, if a little overdone. Hating his part in the theatricals, he reached for Bridge's hand, took his pulse, then used a stethoscope on his chest.

When he thought he'd done enough to convince his audience, he turned to Webster and frowned. 'Looks bad. I think his heart is struggling and he needs to go to hospital. Keep him warm while I go call for an ambulance.'

Webster blew out his cheeks. Frown lines creased his forehead. 'I'll have to inform the governor first. Get his permission.'

'No time for that,' Alex said with deliberate emphasis. 'I'll use the phone in your office before you do. I'll ring for the ambulance, then get a trolley up here to transport him to the loading bay. After that you can ring the governor.'

'It's that urgent, is it? He's that bad?'

'Bad enough not to take a chance. Just look at him.'

'Right,' Webster said, patently pleased that Alex was taking over, that the decision was out of his hands. 'Use the phone. I'll come down in a minute to inform Governor Baker.'

The tall officer who'd waited outside the cell accompanied Alex on his way back to the Webster's office.

'Don't trust him, me,' he opined as they hurried along. 'You sure it's his heart and not in his daft head? He'll be up to some-thing. Mark my words.'

How near he was to the truth shook Alex. This officer knew his man all right so, where Bridge's actions were concerned, the other staff on the wing must be sceptical as well. After the escape the doctor who'd pronounced on the matter would look very naïve and fingers would be pointed in his direction. He shook off the thought, looked the officer up and down in what he hoped was a suitably officious manner.

'Who's the doctor here?' he said. 'Would you take a chance on his dying if you were me?'

The officer, looking sheepish, grunted. 'Don't suppose I would if I were you, but where he's concerned maybe it wouldn't be a bad thing if he snuffed it.'

As they entered Webster's office Alex tried for a withering look. 'And they try to tell me the day of the politically correct prison officer is upon us.'

Keeping his doubts and emotions in check, he called the hospital for an ambulance, then rang the medical centre and asked Janet to arrange for a trolley equipped with oxygen to be brought to the block immediately. The tall officer waited outside. When the business was done, maintaining a sullen silence, no doubt the result of Alex's chastisements, they walked back to Bridge's cell together.

Webster was waiting at the door. Alex nodded to him indi-cating he'd made his calls. Meanwhile Bridge was keeping up the cacophony of moans and groans.

'Two officers will have to accompany him,' Webster stated.

Alex expected that; it was standard practice. He hoped whoever had formed the escape plan had taken account of their presence and that they would be neutralized in a non-violent manner as Bridge had indicated.

Webster continued, 'And we'll have to cuff him to the officers.'

In response, Alex looked at him doubtfully, stroked his chin, pretended he was mulling it over. If the prisoner was cuffed, escape would be much more difficult and the chances of a violent outcome more likely. Alex didn't want that.

'Cuffs would restrict the blood supply, too big a risk in his condition.'

Webster opened his mouth as though to protest, but shut it again thinking better of it. His petulant expression spoke for him; he didn't like his men accompanying a prisoner without restraints.

'Your show, Doctor,' he said, washing his hands of it. 'You're the main man. Look bad if he dies because we restrained him.'

'No cuffs, then.' Even as Alex spoke, his words weighed heavily. Yet events were already in motion and he had to go with them now, do his best to ensure it went smoothly, trust blindly in the plan however nervous that made him.

Two male nurses pushing a trolley equipped with oxygen arrived. Alex went ahead into the cell, kneeled beside Bridge, performed a last, cursory inspection for appearances' sake, then stood aside to let them in. He watched as they lifted Bridge on to the trolley and put the oxygen mask over his mouth.

'Wheel him as gently as possible, lads,' he said, playing the concerned doctor.

Accompanied by the Senior Officer he followed the nurses through corridors and locked doors to the loading bay. Governor Baker, a plump man in his fifties, with only a couple of years to retirement, was waiting for them. He was twiddling with the middle button of his dark suit. He looked overdressed for the bleak surroundings, like a businessman who has strayed from the salubrious ambience of the boardroom to the more prosaic work floor. Detecting his anxiety, Alex felt another surge of conscience. The governor had been kind to him and he was betraying him when all the man wanted in his final working years was a smooth run to retirement; no potential catastrophes, such as an escape, to bring the wrath of higher authorities down on his head when they needed a scapegoat.

His eye fixed on Alex. 'Are you sure?'

Alex nodded. 'I am.'

The governor stopped twiddling with his button. 'Good enough, then. The ambulance is already waiting outside. We'll open the doors as soon as the escorting officers arrive. Where the hell are they?'

'Here, sir.'

Two officers had arrived behind them. Alex recognized one, Officer Clark, a ruddy faced young man whom he knew the prisoners liked because he was firm but fair and would go out of his way to help them. He remembered that in conversation Clark had mentioned he had a young family. The other officer was middle-aged but, other than that his name was Higgins, like the snooker player, he didn't know him. He hoped neither man would choose to play hero today.

'Which hospital are they going to?' the governor inquired of Alex as the Senior Officer briefed the officers.

'South Tees, Governor.'

Alex watched him purse his lips. He knew he was calculating the possibilities, any potential obstructions to a smooth run.

'It'll take about … fifteen minutes. Traffic's not too bad on Marton Road this time of day,' he said.

Simultaneously, they looked down at Bridge on the trolley. The governor nodded at Alex, then raised a hand and the doors swung. The ambulance drove in and two paramedics dressed in green tunics emerged from the back doors. One of them went straight to Bridge and began examining him, while the other addressed Alex and the governor.

'Which of you gentlemen is the doctor?'

Alex stepped forward, told him Bridge was showing signs of

an impending heart attack and needed close observation in hospital.

'Just get him there as quickly as possible,' he added.

The medics got straight to work, wheeling the trolley right up to the back doors of the ambulance. They lifted Bridge on to a stretcher and carried him inside. Clark and Higgins climbed in behind them. As soon as they were all settled, the doors closed and the driver started the engine.

Like the gates of a medieval fortress, the tall doors swung open and the ambulance reversed into the daylight. Alex watched until it sped off. Then the doors started to close shutting out the daylight again. Alex felt something inside him diminishing with the fading light because it was done now and there was no chance of stopping the chain of events he'd helped set in motion. He'd stepped over to join those on the dark side. His greatest fear was for those men in the ambulance, whose safety he'd had to weigh in the balance against his family's safety. God forbid they'd be hurt during the escape. He'd wanted to believe Bridge when he'd said that wouldn't happen but, as the business had unfolded and the reality hit home, he realized his optimism was mainly based on wishful thinking. Would he be able to live with it if anyone was hurt? That was the question which started to nag away at him and which he knew would continue to assail him until this was over.

CHAPTER 15

Bridge figured that the sense of exhilaration as the ambulance accelerated away from the place of his incarceration was better than the high any of his punters had achieved from the drugs he sold them. It had all gone so well. The doc had come through. There were moments he'd doubted he would, when he'd thought he might have an attack of conscience and give him up, in spite of the pressure exerted on him. But it hadn't happened and he was on his way, his freedom so close he could taste it.

He was aware that the paramedics were hovering over him and that the screws were sitting near the doors looking as though they'd rather be somewhere else. Just wait boys, he thought, there'll be plenty of action soon, only you won't like being on the receiving end. Himself, he couldn't wait to be rid of that damn oxygen mask clinging to his face like a blood-sucking alien. He tried to put his discomfort out of mind. Not long now and he'd be out of this tin can, breathing proper fresh air.

Seven minutes into the journey a jolt so violent that even he had not anticipated its force threw him off the bed and dislodged the mask. The paramedics and screws came off much worse, bouncing off the sides of the ambulance like pinballs until they settled in a heap on the floor, limbs entangling in a collective sprawl. In the ominous silence which followed, Bridge heard their moans and groans. It was sweet music to his ears.

'What's happened?' one of the paramedics shouted, holding his head in his hands.

The younger of the screws disentangled himself from the mêlée, stepped over Bridge and peered out of the small window which gave a restricted view into the driver's cabin and of the road in front of the ambulance.

'We've been hit by a van,' he declared. 'The driver's outside staggering about.'

Bridge couldn't help himself. He tore off the mask, laughed and said, 'Send for an ambulance, why don't you?'

The older screw, Higgins, was still on the floor rubbing his arm. He froze mid-motion, stared at the prisoner wondering how he'd revivified all of a sudden. A gleam of suspicion came into his eye.

'Get on your radio right now!' he shouted to Clark. 'This might be—'

The rest of his sentence was drowned in the explosion that blew in the doors. A shock wave shook the ambulance and threw Clark backwards so that he ended up sprawled on top of the others. A shroud of smoke engulfed them all. Bridge heard Higgins cough and splutter and emit a strangulated curse. A little stunned himself, but aware enough to know he had to be ready to move, he lifted a foot off his chest and hauled himself free of the others.

He saw the black-clad figure in a balaclava emerge from the smoke like a devilish spectre from Hell. The figure pointed a shotgun at the entangled bodies on the floor, trying to distinguish one from the other but finding it difficult. A rough voice called out in exasperation.

'Charlie, get outside! Quick man! There's too much smoke. I can't see you.'

Freedom so close now that he could smell it, Bridge crawled. Outside the doors, just visible through the swirling smoke, he could see a patch of blue sky where freedom resided, his freedom. A hand reached down, pulled at his collar. Two eyes peered at him through slits in a balaclava.

'Gotcha, feller!' the rough voice exclaimed.

Bridge started to rise, his eyes fixed on that patch of blue. Yet, to his horror, he couldn't move. Someone was holding his leg, trying to drag him back. Demented, he kicked out with his free leg, but the grip wasn't relinquished, only tightened.

'He's got my ankle,' he screamed looking up at his helper. 'Do something!'

The masked figure turned back, reversed the shotgun, held the barrel. His arm rose high, came down hard. He repeated the action with equal venom. Bridge heard a groan somewhere behind him and felt the grip on his ankle loosen. Leaning on the gunman, he hauled himself upright, staggered to the door. His rescuer helped him down to the ground and leapt out himself.

As soon as he was out two masked men grabbed his arms, hurried him to the front of the ambulance. He was conscious of cars behind the ambulance, drivers and passengers watching with shocked expressions, frozen in their seats as though they were watching a scene from a film.

A silver BMW waited at the side of the road, its engine revving as though it was a restrained beast anxious for release. The men threw Bridge on to the back seat. One of them followed him, the other jumped in the other side. In the same second, the driver slammed his foot down. With a final roar, the beast sprang into action, tyres screeching.

Elated, Bridge laughed, shouted above the roar, 'Good job, boys! Stunning, totally stunning.'

Both men removed their masks. Bridge didn't recognize them, figured they must be men his sister had hired. So far, in his estimation, they'd been full value for money, no matter how much she'd paid.

'We're only half done,' one of the men grunted, glancing through the window over his shoulder for signs of pursuit. 'You be ready to get out soon, Charlie!'

'Soon?' Bridge queried.

He looked out through the side, then the back window. They were bombing down a deserted road, in what looked like an industrial estate. He shot forward as the driver suddenly braked and they stopped abruptly. The doors to a garage on their right swung open. The driver accelerated again and drove inside. As the doors closed behind them, the driver cut the engine. In the silence and semi-darkness, there was a moment of relief after the frenetic speed and tension. Then one of the masked men spoke.

'Out Charlie!'

He did as he was told. There were another two vehicles inside the garage, a Land-Rover and an old Primera. In the dim light he could make out an indistinct figure behind the wheel of the Primera.

One of the men placed a hand on his shoulder. 'We leave you here. You go in the Primera. You already know the driver. He'll look after you.'

Bridge opened his mouth to say something but was cut off. 'Just do it, Charlie. Time counts for all of us.'

In the blink of an eye the three men removed their black attire, changed into casual clothing. Two of them clambered into the Land-Rover while the other opened the garage doors. Then the Land-Rover shot forward out of the garage and the doors closed again, leaving Charlie standing there like an abandoned child.

He started towards the Primera. A thin man, long arms accentuated by a polo-necked jumper, climbed out to greet him. He recognized Bill Fraser, an old acquaintance. In the gloom of the garage his gaunt face and high cheekbones were almost ghoulish. After they'd shaken hands Bridge started for the passenger side but Fraser called him back and opened the boot.

He leaned forward, lifted a panel which hid a space at the back with just enough room to conceal a body.

'Custom made for you,' Fraser said with a sweeping gesture. 'There's a flashlight so you don't get scared in the dark, some sandwiches and a flask of coffee and even a bottle to pee in.'

Bridge groaned his displeasure. 'I ain't going to be in there that long, am I?'

Fraser smiled. Something was amusing him. 'You're going back to prison, mate,' he chortled, 'and you'll just have to grin and bear it.'

Charlie didn't see the joke. For a fleeting moment, he thought Fraser had turned against him, was about to betray him for the bounty on his head.

Fraser laughed at his bemusement. 'Don't worry,' he said, 'it's all part of your sister's plan. Get in, man.'

Charlie frowned. 'Tell me before I do.'

Fraser put a hand on his shoulder. 'I'm going on my regular prison visit to see a pal. Like it always is, this car will be parked in the visitor's car park as near those grey walls as it can get. After the visit, I'll drive the quarter-mile to the shopping mall for my usual leisurely shopping spree. I'll buy myself a meal and, if there's time, I might even pop into the cinema.'

'And I'm in there while you're enjoying yourself?' Bridge moaned. He got it now though. Smiling, he patted the vehicle. 'This is our Trojan horse, ain't it? We're hiding right under the enemy's nose till it cools down a bit.'

'Your sister's bright, Charlie. Trust her. Put up with the confinement 'cos it'll be worth it.'

Feeling better now that he knew the score, Bridge started to climb in. Half-way inside, a thought struck him and he paused.

'How many dead bodies you had in here, Bill?'

'Only two,' Fraser answered, deadpan.

'Make sure I'm not the third, then.'

When Fraser put the panel back in place and closed the boot Bridge was shrouded in darkness. He could feel the torch beside him, was grateful it was there if he felt the need. The worst of it was that he couldn't stretch his legs fully, had to lie with them bent. A few hours like that and he figured rigor mortis could set in. He closed his eyes, hoping he would sleep because that would make the time pass more quickly.

Bridge slept fitfully. The hours passed slowly. There was a buzz knowing that on the first stop, when the engine cut, he was only a few yards from his former residence: one in the eye for the opposition who thought they could hold on to Charlie Bridge. The coffee and sandwiches, wolfed down in torchlight, helped to alleviate the boredom a little.

Then the engine started up again and he was aware that they were driving away from the prison. When Fraser turned on the radio he could just hear it. A newscaster was announcing that the hunt was on for an escaped prisoner. All major roads were being watched. Well, as far as he was concerned, they could watch all they liked. His sister had been too clever for them.

The vehicle soon stopped again. He heard the door slam and resigned himself to another long wait. After what seemed an age, he fell asleep. A noise woke him with a start. Disorientated in the dark, he thought he was in his cell until he realized it was Fraser opening the boot and not some officer doing the rounds. By now his whole body was aching, as though the last hours had been spent confined in a straitjacket.

Fraser's voice reached him, 'How you feeling, Charlie?'

'How do sardines feel?' Bridge grunted. 'At least they got company. How long left in this hole?'

'We're heading towards the moors, all the quiet roads. Your sister will meet us there.'

Behind the panel, Bridge groaned with feeling. 'Another hour?'

'Yeah! But it's for the best. Even if we're stopped, they ain't likely to find you if you keep your mush shut. I've got no record, Charlie, so they won't suspect me.'

'Let's do it then.'

The journey was tedious. At last, Fraser stopped and cut the engine. Bridge figured they must have arrived and felt a surge of excitement at the prospect of being released from his alternative prison.

He heard Fraser get out, slam the door and open the boot. When the panel was removed, Fraser reached in to help him. His legs felt unsteady when he stood and his back muscles protested. Leaning against the vehicle for support, he waited until a semblance of normality returned to his body.

The moon was behind them. Clouds hovered, guardians of its silver light, threatening to obscure it. A breeze tugged at the trees on either side. Stars twinkled in flirtation with the darkness. Bridge grinned his satisfaction. This was what he called freedom; no more artificial light, no grey walls, just that fresh breeze on your face and the universe looking down on you.

Fraser pointed. Bridge saw a car further down the lane. Its lights were off but he could make out a figure standing beside it and waving at them. He knew it was Bella.

Fraser patted him on the back and shut the boot. 'Get going and thank your sister for her hard work.'

Bridge grinned ruefully, 'Not to mention the money she's paid out to arrange all this.'

'There's always that,' Fraser stated. 'It took money to get you out. But you already know that.'

'Way of the world. Good job we've plenty to spare,' Bridge said and started to walk down the lane towards his sister.

Bella held out her arms in welcome and embraced her brother.

'Masterly!' he said, pulling away to scrutinize her. 'Up to your usual standards.'

She smiled, broke away, reached inside the car, brought out a long coat which she handed to him.

'Put this on, brother. We need to hide those stinking prison clothes just in case we're stopped, which is extremely doubtful now.'

He did as he was told and then went to the passenger door while she climbed in the driver's side. When he was settled she started the engine, switched the headlights on and drove slowly down the lane.

Rubbing the stiffness which lingered in his arms and legs, he said, 'Where to now – Spain, Italy, South America?'

Bella's eyes flickered in his direction. 'Charlie dear, I'm your sister not your personal holiday rep. You know they'll be watching the airports and ports. You're going to have to be patient and trust me. I've a place to hide you for now – not very salubrious but I'll be close by and able to keep an eye on you. When I'm convinced the search has cooled off, we'll move on.'

Bridge hid his disappointment. He was impatient to leave the country but he knew his sister was a wise one, less impulsive than he was. She'd never let him down, always had his best interest at heart. He was lucky the bond formed during their itinerant childhood was so strong. Best then to trust her good brain and survival instincts.

'How long before we leave the country?'

'Probably weeks. Then it's sunshine all the way for us.'

'Can't grumble,' he said and leaned back, forcing himself to relax. 'I'm out. That's what counts, eh!'

Bella took one hand off the steering wheel, touched his arm in an affectionate gesture.

'Poor you,' she cooed. 'Locked up with all those sex offenders.'

'Wouldn't wish it on an ordinary, decent criminal,' he said, stretching.

A silver shaft of moonlight touched his sister's cheek. Bridge noticed her perfect teeth as her mouth drew back in a smile.

'What does that make you, brother?'

He laughed. 'Extraordinary and indecent. It runs in the family, of course. Didn't you know that?'

She joined his laughter as a cloud hid the moon.

Chapter 16

The day after the escape, Alex was sitting in his office with a hangover. He felt like a condemned man awaiting his execution. Yesterday, only an hour or so after the news came through, the prison rumour mill started grinding away; he'd heard various theories from Joyce, who'd heard them from prison officers. Trying to ferret out whether anyone had been hurt, he'd pressed her for substantial details but she hadn't known any.

Last night, while he waited for the news on the television, to anaesthetize his conscience he'd drunk himself silly. There'd been a marked absence of detail in the reports, other than an outdated photograph of a smiling Charlie Bridge which had made him want to put his boot to the television and smash the image to smithereens. The whisky hadn't helped and failed to obliterate pessimistic thoughts about what wasn't being said in those reports. He expected a home visit from the police at any time but it never came. Maybe they wouldn't tie him in with the escape, but deep down knew it was too much to hope that suspicion wouldn't fall his way. He figured the police must be too concerned with the search in these early stages.

The summons he was expecting came an hour into his working day and was almost welcome because he was certain he'd hear something at last to fill the vacuum of doubt which was making him nervous. Liberally dosed with peppermints, which he hoped would hide any smell lingering on his breath from his drinking bout last night, he made his way to the governor's office as commanded. Composing himself, he knocked on the door and, when a voice called out, entered with a prayer that no real harm had been done.

Governor Baker was sitting behind his desk, his face as grey as the suit he was wearing. Black shadows under his eyes that looked like tiny birds' wings told of a sleepless night. His shoulders, normally military-straight, were hunched inwards so that he looked shrunken. Another man was sitting on the governor's right. He was bulky, his shoulders fitting a dark suit almost to bursting. Coal-black hair, trimmed short, gave emphasis to blue eyes which, fixed rigidly on Alex, made him uncomfortable as he crossed the room.

'Take a seat, Doctor Macdonald,' Baker said, his voice too formal for Alex's liking as he gestured to the chair in front of his desk. 'This is Detective Inspector Johnson. He's investigating yesterday's escape and would like to ask a few questions.'

Alex and the detective nodded at each other. There was something about the detective he didn't like. Or was that just a manifestation of his own guilt surfacing?

'You know Charlie Bridge escaped, Doctor?' the detective said, leaning forward.

'I heard it on the radio and saw it television.'

'And you were the one who sent him out of here – to hospital?'

There was just enough of a whiff of accusation in the way the detective said it. Was it to disconcert him? Did he know something? Suspect something? Or was it just a policeman's acquired manner?

'I suspected a heart problem. His pulse was racing and he was in pain. I concluded he needed to go to hospital post haste.'

The detective's tongue prodded the inside of his cheek,

worked its way round with slow deliberation as though searching the crevices. His eyes had never left Alex's face.

'Because you wanted to be on the safe side. Proper procedure and such. Covering yourself,' Johnson's sardonic tone and manner implied more than the meaning of the words themselves.

'I was being professional,' Alex said, ashamed of his own hypocrisy, doing his best not to let it show.

'But Bridge had come to see you two days earlier complaining of pains. That's right isn't it?'

Alex hesitated, fractionally. Where was this going?

'That's correct.'

Johnson lowered his eyebrows, 'But on that occasion you did nothing, Didn't prescribe anything. Just ... talked.'

A bead of sweat gathered on Alex's forehead. To him, it felt like an excrescence of his guilt. Not wanting to draw attention to it, he had to resist the temptation to wipe it away.

'On that occasion, I examined him thoroughly and couldn't find a problem. I believed he had indigestion, a bad case of indigestion which would pass.'

The detective angled his head, scratched at his temple and shut one eye, like an imitation of Peter Falk in *Columbo*.

'Clearly your professional opinion was wrong.'

The words, intimating incompetence, hung on the air. Alex glanced at the governor but his face was impassive, his eyes looking right through him. He met the policeman's gaze again. The smile lurking at the corner of his mouth was like an assassin's, cold and knowing.

'These things can never be precise. Perhaps on the day it was indigestion or perhaps it was an indication of heart trouble on the way.'

'Yes, of course – perhaps. We hear that word a lot in my profession as it happens.'

Alex cringed inwardly. This detective was a master of indi-
rectness, of speaking in a way that implied other connotations.
Maybe it was his way of goading you, making you lose control
so you'd say more than you should. If it was, Alex wasn't going
to fall for it, no matter how guilt-ridden he was feeling.

The detective continued. 'Did you prescribe anything for his
indigestion?'

Alex thought quickly. 'I believe I gave him a spoonful of
medicine.'

'Must be good stuff,' the detective snorted. 'According to the
escorting officer, he walked back to the block with a spring in his
step, like a man who has just struck gold. The opposite of the
way he came to you, he said.'

Alex decided attack was the best form of defence. 'Are you
implying something here, Inspector?'

Shaking his head, the detective shrugged. 'Merely wishing *my*
doctor was so … productive.'

Alex couldn't read his expression. Again, the words were
invested with just enough sarcasm to distort what was said and
imply other, more sinister, possibilities. Was he on a fishing
expedition, or did he know something?

Alex's eyes flitted to the governor. His eyes seemed as glazed
as those of the addicts under his charge. Silence swelled to
bursting point in the room. Wanting to be out of there, Alex took
the initiative.

'Was there anything else?'

'Later maybe.' The detective grunted. 'What about you,
Governor? Any questions?'

Baker's body gave a little jolt as though he was dreaming he
was somewhere else, was reluctant to return. He didn't speak,
just shook his head.

Alex stood up. His insides were churning from Johnson's
prying and the governor's haunted, broken look, which brought

home his own guilt. But there was something he wanted to ask, had postponed under the barrage of awkward questions from the detective. At the door, he turned sheepishly and addressed the governor.

'Was anyone … hurt?'

The governor looked down at his desk and, dredging for his words, said, 'Officer Clark received blows to his head. Presently he's in a coma. We're all very concerned.'

Johnson couldn't resist the opportunity. 'We wondered if you'd ask. It may interest you to know, Doctor, that after the officer was struck Bridge made a remarkable recovery from his heart problem and leapt like Lazarus from his bed.'

The announcement shocked Alex. He stood there realizing those words about nobody getting hurt had meant nothing to the gangster. A weight gathered inside him threatening to root him to the spot for ever. What he had been fearing most had come to pass; a man was badly hurt, might die because he, Alex, had helped Bridge. Why hadn't he just stood up to the gangster? Yet how could he have with his family in danger? Had he really had a choice? In his torment and confusion hatred for Bridge gathered momentum and he was overwhelmed by a burgeoning urge to strike back, make him suffer—

'Doctor!' The governor's voice, thin and reedy, brought him right back to the moment. 'If only you'd….'

He didn't need to finish because the implication was clear enough. He suspected Alex of, at least, incompetence. If that was in Governor Baker's mind, no doubt others would be thinking it too. The detective inspector would be no exception. He tried to find something to say but nothing would come because he was guilty and nothing could change that. Instead, he just opened the door and walked out, his head hanging low.

Like a zombie, aware of nothing and nobody, he made his way back to his office. For the rest of the day he went through the motions of doing his work, his mind wandering but consumed by guilt and a burning hatred of the man who had used him and brought him down. Was it his imagination or paranoia that his staff seemed already to have distanced themselves from him, that he could see something new in their eyes, even in the imperturbable Joyce's? How much did they know? It was a great relief when he finished for the day, but he was aware that his mood wouldn't be assuaged by a change of scenery because his part in the damage to Clark had embedded itself in his soul.

CHAPTER 17

Guilt-ridden days and nights passed. Life was a living hell for Alex, the nights barely relieved by the increasingly familiar solace of the whisky bottle, the days allowing no reprieve at all. He managed to drag himself to work each day, go through the motions, but self-disgust lay heavily on his shoulders, sneering at his attempts to pretend he could go on as normal, that everything was the same. Of his own staff, only Joyce treated him in anything more than a perfunctory fashion. Yet, even in her eyes, he could see the conflict between loyalty and doubts about him. Twice, during those days, she had cause to reprimand him for careless, uncharacteristic errors; she told him that if he wasn't himself, he should go home and rest. In return he had snapped at her about minding her business.

Worse than anything was the attitude of the prison officers towards him. Wherever he went he could feel their eyes following, was aware of them avoiding his when he happened to look in their direction, of their conspiratorial whisperings. Blatant contempt, in the faces of those who had already judged him, was the hardest thing to take because he couldn't deny it was justified. Clearly the word was out that he was the one responsible for Bridge being in the ambulance when, judging by his miraculous recovery during the escape, he was perfectly fit. The popular Officer Clark was paying the forfeit and Alex himself, the doctor, because of his perceived incompetence, was an obvious scapegoat.

On the morning of the fifth day after the escape, Joyce knocked on his office door and he called her in. She looked worried.

'The governor's rung down,' she said. 'He wants to see you immediately.'

'Put him off will you. I've work to do.'

From under arched eyebrows, she gave him a stern look, the one that must have caused many a junior nurse trepidation over the years. It captured his attention.

'You have to go. After all, he is the boss of this prison and it sounded like an urgent command to me.'

Alex sighed, pushed his chair back and ran a hand through his dishevelled hair. 'Oh, very well,' he said impatiently.

'No need to take it out on me,' she snapped at him. 'I'm just the messenger.'

Before he had a chance to apologize she had closed the door behind her. He immediately regretted that he had offended her again but, when he went out after her, she'd disappeared.

On the way to see the governor all the black thoughts he'd been holding at bay rose up like demons. The possibility that they had discovered evidence of his part in the escape was one. But the worst was the depressing thought that perhaps Clark had died leaving a widow and two kids behind.

His heart beat like a drum and invisible forces pulled his stomach as he entered Baker's office. He'd half-expected the police to be there, so it was a measure of relief when only the governor was present. Baker was seated at his desk. His face was expressionless as he watched Alex cross the room. For a moment Alex dispatched his demons, dared to hope. Perhaps he had only been called here to discuss work matters after all.

The governor's demeanour soon disposed of that possibility. First, he didn't invite Alex to sit down, let him stand before him like a recalcitrant schoolboy due for a severe rebuke. Secondly,

Alex could detect a certain distaste, as though an unpleasant odour had entered his room and he wanted rid of it as soon as possible.

'I'll get straight to the point,' Baker announced, his voice cold and formal, eyes never leaving Alex's face as he shuffled papers on his desk. 'I have evidence here of your gross incompetence, Doctor Macdonald. This leaves me no choice other than to suspend you from your duties forthwith and for an as yet indeterminate period.'

Alex thought the game was up, that they were on to him and, curiously, he felt some sense of relief because it would mean he could drop the pretence. Yet, logically, wouldn't the police be here to arrest him if that were so?

'Exactly what have I done?' he asked, keeping his voice as calm as he could.

'I'm coming to that,' Baker said, maintaining his detachment. 'My decision was based on a security check made last night. The security personnel found the door to the pharmacy unlocked and discovered that you were the last one to draw the key. As you well know, it was a dangerous breach. Anyone could have walked in and stolen drugs.'

Alex felt himself flush but was unable to defend himself. Without a doubt, he'd been struggling just to get through the days, his mind preoccupied. Though he couldn't exactly remember leaving the pharmacy unlocked, the accusation was probably true, given his state of mind and inability to concentrate properly. No doubt the amount of booze he'd been consuming had contributed.

'Furthermore and probably more dangerous,' Baker continued, 'a pair of scissors, traceable to your office, were found in one of the cells where an inmate had secreted them away. The same scissors were marked with your initials and were missing from your cupboard, to which only you hold the key.'

Alex opened his mouth to speak but nothing would come out because he knew he must have been careless on both counts. What could he say? Both charges were serious enough for him to be dismissed from his job. It was an inevitability, in fact, and he'd only himself to blame. The irony was, when Bridge's gangsters first entrapped him, he'd co-operated because he'd wanted to keep his job and reputation. Now both were forfeit. Worse, he had the added worry and guilt about young Clark. How much worse could his life and luck get?

'Do you want to say anything?' the governor asked, his tone and heavy frown implying that he had little sympathy to offer.

For a second Alex was tempted to tell Baker the whole story, relieve his conscience. But then the police would go after Bridge's people and, if the criminal suspected he'd talked, his gang might retaliate against his own family and Gloria. That apart, he'd have to face charges himself; he might be able to face his punishment but he knew it could devastate his daughter.

'Nothing,' he grunted. 'No excuses. I made mistakes for which I'm sorry.'

Baker leaned back, entwined his fingers on the desk. 'Very well. You'll hear from us in due course.'

Nothing more was said until, head down, Alex walked to the door. His hand was on the doorknob when the governor called after him.

'You'll be relieved, no doubt, to hear that Clark has woken from his coma.'

To Alex, at that moment, those words seemed like a blessing and he felt as though a great weight had lifted off him. Someone up there loved him after all; no permanent damage had been done to anyone. He turned to face the governor.

'Thank God for that!'

'Unfortunately,' Baker continued, 'his left arm is paralysed.

They don't think it will improve. He'll receive compensation but he'll lose his job and his working life will never be the same.'

Alex's relief disintegrated. He realized the governor's words were more to do with blaming him for his dubious misdiagnosis than a compensatory gesture. Without a word he left the room and made his way back to the medical centre. He felt completely defeated but, by the time he arrived back at his own office, his hatred for the criminal who had used him and hurt Clark had mushroomed. More than that, a desire to hit back had started to flourish in a part of him that he thought he had buried when he'd become a healer.

After he'd gathered his personal possessions together, he put them in a bag and called Joyce into the office. She entered unsmiling and he could see she was still smarting from his rudeness earlier.

'I'm sorry,' he said. 'I was out of order.'

'Forget it. Just get back to being yourself.' She arched an eyebrow when she saw the bag with his possessions on the desk.

He cleared his throat. 'Joyce, I've been suspended. I don't think I'll be back. I'd like to say I've appreciated all your help.'

'What's happened?' she asked, obviously bemused. 'I've heard gossip but this....'

He told her about the pharmacy and the scissors. 'I haven't a leg to stand on,' he said. 'It was me being careless and they can't allow security to be compromised.'

She cast her eyes downwards. 'There's been something wrong with you for a long time, hasn't there?'

He was tempted to tell her about Bridge. Instead, he said, 'I've had terrible trouble in my life.'

She bit her bottom lip. 'I knew there was something. If I can help—'

'Nobody can,' he interrupted. 'But thanks.'

He picked up his bag and made his way to the door. When he was on the threshold, Joyce called his name.

'I believe you're a good man,' she said, 'in spite of what they've been saying.'

He smiled sadly. 'It's easy even for a good man to slip, Joyce.'

CHAPTER 18

The previous day Gloria had arrived back from York. She'd rung him every night while she was away. He'd managed to put up a front during their conversations but tonight was different. He knew his mood would filter through so he sat her down, told her he'd been suspended and why, adding he'd had things on his mind which had made him careless. She looked at him with her big blue eyes and, in a sympathetic voice, said something must be wrong with his health, suggested, without any sense of irony, that he should see a doctor. Maybe if they discovered he was ill they'd forgive him his lapses and he'd keep his job. In bed that night she held him in her arms, spoke soothing words and he was glad that at least someone was there for him, that he wasn't all alone.

Next morning he was up early and forced himself to drive into Glaisdale, the nearest small village, to collect a paper and buy some groceries. As he drove the black mood hit with full battalions. All his hard work and sacrifices to become a doctor seemed to have been in vain. How would he find employment now? Perhaps there'd be a job for him somewhere, but it wouldn't be easy to find it if the reasons for his current plight became known. And how was he going to tell Liz and Ann? They'd be ashamed of him, wouldn't they?

Even those black thoughts paled besides his torment over Officer Clark's plight. That young man had a family as well; they would be suffering. Like an evil genie released in his brain, Bridge's face with its supercilious grin floated into Alex's consciousness. The criminal, the instigator of all this trouble, became the focus of his pent-up rage. How he wished he could make him pay?

He carried the groceries into the kitchen and dumped them on the table, calling out Gloria's name. There was no answer. He thought she must have gone upstairs so he slipped his jacket off and headed to the living-room for a quick nip of whisky before she came down.

Gloria wasn't upstairs. She was in the living room. He saw her through the open door and halted mid-stride. She was sitting bolt upright, unnaturally so, on a hard backed chair in the centre of the room, sideways on to Alex. Her face was immobile. Sensing there was something wrong, he started forward without a moment's hesitation.

When he entered the room, he saw the ropes binding her to the chair. He halted, his body tensing. From the corner of his eye, he saw a movement. His head swung round. A man he didn't recognize was standing by the window. He had a gun in his hand and there was something familiar about his stance.

It took a minute because the hair was dyed grey and the intruder had the start of a beard. But the arrogant stance and the supercilious grin clinched it. Alex's heart pounded. Charlie Bridge in the flesh; the last man he'd expected to see here. His confusion rooted him to the spot. Questions raced through his brain. Why wasn't this man right out of his life by now? What could he possibly want here?

'Surprise! Surprise!' Bridge said, brandishing the gun. 'Guess who?'

Alex swallowed hard, recovered some composure. He was conscious that Gloria was looking at him now.

He mumbled, 'Has he hurt you?'

'No!' Her voice was strong enough but carried a hint of rebuke and her eyes seemed to be accusing him.

He faced Bridge, fired questions in temper. 'What are you doing here? Why is she tied up?'

'Now, now, Doc,' Bridge said lazily. 'Calmness is called for here, like when you're operating or dealing with a crazy patient like me.'

'You're crazy coming here,' Alex snapped back.

Bridge pulled a face. 'Don't go all self-righteous on me, not when we've got history together.'

Alex glanced at Gloria. Bridge continued: 'Don't worry, Gloria and me have had a little chat, a little update. She's really surprised you didn't tell her about our arrangement. She's disappointed in you. I know women. I can tell.'

Alex sat on his temper. The bastard had told Gloria he'd helped him escape. Who else might he tell? Where was it all going to end?

'This wasn't part of our arrangement. You said I'd never see you again. Just what do you want that's worth the risk of coming here?'

'Method in my madness, old son.' He walked to the window, gestured with the weapon in the direction of the run-down barn. 'It wasn't exactly comfortable for a man of my impeccable taste living out there, not your actual Savoy, but it served its purpose. Thing is, it'll be easier to move by now.'

Alex's temper flared. He felt more used than ever. Bridge had had the cheek to hide on his property. Gaining an inch, he had taken miles. And he was still here taking liberties because he figured he had a hold over him.

'I shouldn't have believed a word that came out of your evil mouth.'

Bridge laughed. 'Don't spoil things. No need, is there? Not when you've mother and daughter to consider, not to mention the pretty lady here.'

Alex didn't need reminding. It was all that stopped him

taking his chances and flying at the gangster. Instead, he glared across the space between them.

'Why did you harm that officer? You said nobody would get hurt. It was understood.'

Bridge snorted, 'Get real, Doc. Did you really believe something like that wouldn't happen? Or did you want to believe it? That screw was foolish enough to try it on and he got what he deserved. End of story. Move on, man.'

Inside, Alex fumed, but he couldn't find an answer because there was an element of truth in the gangster's words. He had wanted to believe it would be all right, had pushed aside the fact that he was dealing with violent men. But there could be no doubt about it; he was guilty by association and therefore tainted. As a result, Bridge's hold over him was stronger than ever.

Bridge stepped away from the window. 'Darling Gloria is going to drive me away from this country retreat suitable only for social pariahs. But don't worry, she'll drop me somewhere and be back before you know it. All you have to do is wait a few hours and not get panicky.'

'Why don't you drive yourself?' Alex came back at him, fearing for Gloria's safety. 'Or take me instead of her?'

'A man and a woman out for a country drive is much less suspicious and I couldn't be sure of you, Doc. You might go Rambo on me. Knowing your lady love is with me you'll wait here like a good boy, won't you?'

Alex looked at Gloria. Her face was expressionless. At least she seemed to be in control, no sign of fear.

'If anything happens to her—'

'Nothing will unless you kick off. Like I said, she'll be back and unharmed. Now be a good lad and untie her. My patience is wearing thin.'

Alex concluded he had no choice but to obey. Bridge was the

one holding the gun and all the other aces. He worked the knots holding Gloria loose. When their eyes met he could see no fear in hers, just what he interpreted as a calm understanding that they had to comply with Bridge's demands. When he'd finished he helped her up and faced the gangster.

'Over here, my dear,' Bridge commanded, sickening Alex with the confident mock familiarity, which seemed to give him a kick.

Without so much as a glance at Alex and betraying not a flicker of emotion, as though today's happenings were an everyday occurrence, Gloria crossed the room and stood next to Bridge. Even in his distressed state of mind Alex marvelled at her composure. He wanted to tell her everything would be all right, that he was sorry, but when he saw the triumphant grin on Bridge's face he held back.

Bridge took her elbow and, pointing the gun at Alex, walked her to the living room door.

'End of our acquaintanceship, Doc.' he said. 'No more guest appearances. Thanks for your co-operation and the use of that old barn. It meant the world to me and I'm off to see the world soon. Hope it works out for you and Gloria when she gets back.' Bridge winked. 'The truth had to out, Doc. I did you a favour when you think of it.'

Held on a tight leash by his fear for Gloria and the people nearest to him, not to mention the weapon Bridge was pointing at him, Alex remained where he was and watched them leave the room. From the kitchen came the sound of Bridge's laughter, a last dying echo of the criminal's triumph over him.

He watched the car set off, then sank into a chair, cursing his enforced inertia and the man who was responsible. He only hoped Bridge would do what he said and release Gloria, let her return to him unharmed, because he was powerless to help her now.

He drank enough but resisted the urge to get drunk. Exhausted by events, he almost fell asleep, revived when he heard what he thought was another echo of Bridge's mocking laughter, then realized it was just the cawing of crows from nearby woodland. Wishing time away, he kept looking at the clock but its hands seemed stubbornly unyielding. What if Bridge harmed Gloria? The thought was unbearable. In temper, he threw the whisky bottle across the room. Eventually he lost the battle to stay awake.

A noise like a gunshot woke him with a jolt. As he leapt out of the chair, he glanced at the clock. Four hours had passed since Gloria had been taken. Knocking into the furniture, he ran across the room, through the hallway and into the kitchen. He opened the back door and hurled himself over the step into the fresh air. The car was back in the yard and Gloria was striding towards him. She looked as healthy and vibrant as a model bouncing along the catwalk. He realized it was the car door slamming he'd heard, breathed a sigh of relief and sucked in a lungful of fresh air.

'Gloria, thank God....'

She was close enough for him to see her eyes. They were like cold, blue stones, no feeling there. Taken aback, he still managed to open his arms to embrace her but she brushed past him and entered the house, leaving him there with outstretched arms like a posed figure in a painting. He wondered why he'd expected anything else after what he'd done.

Wary of her mood, he followed her into the living-room where he found her at the drinks cabinet pouring a brandy. She slugged it down, hands surprisingly steady considering her ordeal. She kept her back turned, as though she was gaining time to rehearse what to say. At last, with a heave of her shoulders, she spun round to face him, her expression as adamantine as her cold eyes.

'How could you?' she screeched, her composure vanishing, hatred in her eyes now. 'How could you live a lie all that time?'

Shocked by the venom of her attack, he forced himself to hold her gaze. 'They threatened to hurt those close to me if I didn't help. What could I have done?'

'You didn't tell me I was in danger just being here with you. You just didn't care, did you?'

She slammed her glass down, slumped in an armchair and hunched up, withdrawing into herself, pushing him out. Alex moved closer, reached out tentatively to touch her shoulder in a sympathetic gesture. She knocked his hand away as though it was a vile intruder in her personal space.

Hurt, he said, 'I thought you would be safer with me, that if he wanted to he could find you anywhere. I thought I could protect you. I thought it best not to worry you—'

'You thought,' she scoffed, eyes sparking. 'You thought about yourself, not me. That's what you did. Don't pretend you were trying to be noble. You've made a big enough fool of me already.'

Alex didn't know how to answer. He'd never seen her like this and it didn't seem the time to argue his case. Whatever he said would be consumed in that furnace of resentment towards him blazing away inside her.

She pounced on his hesitation, snapped at him. 'He told me everything, right from the start, enjoyed telling me. All that sordid business in the hotel. He made a meal of that. You kept that from me all right. Too ashamed were you, Alex?'

'I was set up, Gloria. They drugged me. It was all part of their plan, for God's sake.'

Gloria wasn't listening. She pushed her red hair back and continued her rant.

'And you – helped him escape. That makes you a criminal. My God, I've been living with a criminal.'

'I'm no criminal,' he protested, arms splayed in a gesture of innocence. 'They had me trapped, woman. I had no choice. They threatened to hurt—'

'There's always a choice,' she yelled. 'Like a fool you took the wrong one.'

Her words found his soft underbelly because he already felt a hundred times a fool for believing Bridge. He realized that whatever he said was a waste of time because she'd clearly made up her mind. It dawned on him too, that if Gloria was seeing it that way, then others, not as close to him, would as well. Maybe only a few people would understand the pressure he was under when his family's safety had been threatened.

Gloria wasn't finished with him. As though a wind might arise from nowhere and blow her away, she was gripping the arms of the chair so tightly her knuckles were showing pure white.

'What do you think it was like being tied up like that and not knowing if he would kill me? Then being forced to drive him, with the same thought going round and round in my head.'

Her words were like a whiplash laid across his back. He winced inwardly imagining what it must have been like for her.

Gruffly, he said, 'He didn't hurt you, did he?'

Her cold eyes, like jewels suddenly capturing the sunlight, flashed in his direction.

'No thanks to you, you moron.'

He hung his head. His voice travelled through a labyrinth of doubt to emerge eventually in a hoarse whisper.

'Look – I'm sorry.'

In answer, she propelled herself out of the chair. Throwing her hair back, she looked at him brimful of disdain.

'No way can I stay here. Not after what's happened. I can't trust you and I'd be terrified of it happening again. I'm going upstairs to pack.'

She marched to the door, slammed it behind her on the way out. Alex, rendered helpless by his own sense of defeat and guilt, stood and stared after her. He'd had so many blows recently that Gloria's decision carried an air of inevitability about it. How could he blame her for going? Looking at it from her point of view, how could she stay?

When he heard her come downstairs he was going to offer to carry her case to the car but thought better of it; she'd made it clear enough she didn't want anything to do with him. Maybe she'd come round to seeing his point of view eventually, but he doubted it, given her hostility.

He watched from the window as she put the case in the boot and climbed into the driver's seat. Without a backward glance she started the engine and drove off. Alex watched the car disappearing down the track, then came away from the window with tears in his eyes.

For a long time he just lay on the couch nursing mental wounds, brooding on his misfortunes. His life had become a catalogue of disasters. He'd lost his job, lost Gloria and was totally alone, not to mention the damaged prison officer. The man responsible for all that was running free, didn't possess a conscience to haunt him. The injustice fostered a desire for revenge in Alex and an old fighting madness that he thought had gone for ever began to stir. But what had changed really? What could he do to make Bridge pay for what he had done without risking others?

CHAPTER 19

Ali Hussein stepped out of the car and surveyed the building. The quietness here was so different from the noise of the town, his own habitat. He wondered if the locals lived the peaceful existence it implied. In the case of Doctor Alexander Macdonald, the man he hoped to see, he doubted it somehow, not in recent days anyway.

'Wait in the car,' he told the son who had driven him here, and walked up to the door.

Nobody answered his first knock so he tried again and waited. It took a long time but eventually the door swung open and a tall man with dishevelled hair and two days' bristle on his chin stared out at him with expressionless eyes. He looked as though he had just emerged from hibernation.

'Doctor Macdonald?' Hussein queried.

Alex nodded. 'That's me.'

'Then may I come in and have a word? There is a matter that could be of mutual interest I'd like to discuss.'

Alex's head lolled back. He looked warily at his visitor.

'I'm in no mood for salesmen,' he grunted. 'You've caught me at a bad time.'

He was about to close the door but Hussein said hastily, 'The matter concerns Charles Bridge. Does that interest you?'

Alex blinked rapidly. His brow knitted into a frown. There was suddenly more life in his eyes.

'A policeman, are you? Why didn't you just say so?'

Momentarily amused by that mistaken perception, Hussein smiled.

'Hardly! I am in fact the owner of a restaurant in Middlesbrough. But I have other interests, which are not in the public eye.'

'You're a friend of Bridge,' Alex said, eyeing him distastefully, body tensing.

'Far from it,' Hussein answered. 'If you'll be so good as to let me tell you my tale, you'll know how Bridge stands with me.'

Alex hesitated a moment longer, then made up his mind. He stepped back from the door, opened it wide and made a vague gesture with his hand, indicating that Hussein should enter. The visitor followed his host into the living-room and they both sat down in armchairs.

In the heart of his home Alex suddenly looked more alert, lost the faraway look in his eyes. It was replaced by a wary inquisitiveness about Hussein's reason for being here.

Without fuss, Hussein began: 'I have contacts in prison. They tell me things that go on inside if they think I might be interested.'

Alex interrupted, a touch scornfully, 'Things like the price of heroin? Or am I being presumptuous?'

'Nothing like that,' Hussein came back at him, his expression darkening. 'Other things, like the rumour that you were part of Bridge's escape plan, that you lied and said he had a heart attack on the day he escaped. Apparently many of the prison officers suspect that you were an accomplice.'

'You must be a policeman.' Alex stated sarcastically, his face angry. 'Only a policeman would feel he had the authority, or the effrontery, to say that to me in my own house.'

'You must forgive my bluntness,' Hussein retorted. 'What I am is a father who holds Bridge responsible for his daughter's death and wishes revenge. If you can tell me anything it will go no further than this room. I promise you.'

Alex's first instinct was to tell him to leave but there was something he saw in the man's expression, perhaps a reflection of his own melancholy, that curbed it.

'You say Bridge was responsible for your daughter's death?'

Hussein's eyes took on a distracted look, as though he was wrestling with the reality of what had happened even as he spoke.

'Bridge and his sister got my daughter hooked on heroin. The sister procured her for her brother with pretended affection. She lived with them both until Bridge grew tired of her. Then they threw her out on to the streets where she killed herself with a massive overdose.'

'I'm sorry to hear that,' Alex said, moved to sympathy, knowing how he would have felt if it had been his own daughter.

Hussein gave a little shudder. With an effort, he gathered himself and continued.

'One of my contacts heard Bridge on the phone in the prison. Apparently his exact words were that "the doctor would come round in the end" so I felt there could be some substance in those rumours. I admit it is flimsy evidence but I am trying hard to find Bridge and I had to come to you.'

Alex crossed his arms. 'Why would I admit it to you if it were true?'

Hussein thought for a moment. 'Understand this, Doctor. I have no interest in what you did, or did not do, or in what happens to you. I only want to find Bridge and am hoping you may know something to help me find him.'

'And you intend to kill him if you find him?'

'Don't doubt it. In my life I have done wrong, broken laws but I have never dealt in drugs, nor harmed anyone physically who did not strike the first blow. This man has. He deserves to die.'

From the determined look in Hussein's eye, Alex didn't doubt he would kill Bridge. He understood, too, the power of his emotions. If Bridge had hurt Ann he would be feeling equally vengeful, would want to kill the gangster with his bare hands. It was that kindred feeling which made him decide it would be safe to open up.

'Bridge threatened my family,' he said with a regretful sigh. 'I had to do exactly what he told me to help him escape. I bitterly regret my part but I feel I had no choice. Truly I feel for you over what he did to your daughter but there is nothing I know about him that would help you find him. I was hardly his confidant.'

Hussein dropped his eyes, stared at the carpet, disappointment engulfing his body like an invisible cloak.

'You can think of nothing, no clue where he might be hiding?'

'Like I say, I was just a pawn in his game. He gave nothing like that away. I hate him as much as you. If there was anything, I'd gladly tell you, but I'm afraid I'm no use to you.'

Hussein lifted his eyes, their laserlike intensity piercing any barriers until they reached the core of Alex's being, his soul, where only truth could reside in pure form. Their power subsided when he found no evasions and his expression softened. He nodded his head and rose from the chair. Reaching into his pocket, he took out a business card and placed it on the coffee table.

'If you recall anything at all, please ring me, Doctor. Even a small, seemingly insignificant fact, may help. My arm can stretch a long way if it has to.'

Alex stood up and faced him. 'If anything comes to mind, I'll do that.'

Hussein crossed the room. Alex followed him out to the door. He turned and shook Alex's hand.

'Thank you, Doctor,' he said, his eyes sad now. 'I wish I had protected my family the way you have yours. Don't ever doubt you did the right thing. The consequences of neglecting to do so are hard to live with, believe me.'

'I'm not so sure I did the right thing,' Alex replied. 'There comes a point where men like Bridge have to be faced down or they just go on damaging lives.'

Hussein's features set hard. 'Precisely, and his time is coming.'

Alex watched him cross the yard to the car where his son had waited patiently. Before he climbed in, he called out:

'Ring me if you remember anything.'

Alex waved him off, shut the door and returned to the living-room where he sank into the same chair. It had been a strange visit and one that had left him feeling a fraction better than before. He knew the reason was that Hussein, a father who had lost his daughter because of Bridge, was one person who under-stood the pressure he had been under and concurred with his actions. Hussein had sparked something inside him, too, had blown on the embers of the fire, made him realize that, in spite of his guilty feelings, he had to do something about Bridge or go under himself and be no use to anybody any more. He'd spent too much time brooding about losing Gloria. He'd have to get a grip, face the fact that what had happened had put a chasm between them and she'd never return. End of the day, he'd have to get a life or go under himself.

Middlesbrough late at night, a few stragglers on the streets. Eddie decided one more fare and he'd knock off. The station was just coming into view and three women stepped out from under its arches. Like actresses emerging into the stage spot-light, they were caught in the orange glow of a streetlight. He figured they could be ladies of the night because the vicinity of the station was a known haunt for prostitutes. Their short skirts and short-sleeved blouses, inappropriate for the cold night, fitted the customary image.

One of women hailed his cab. He decided to ignore her because, from previous experience of working girls, he knew they could be a nuisance especially if they'd had poor remuneration for a nightshift, sometimes refusing to pay him.

He was almost past when he caught a glimpse of the dark-haired girl standing next to the blonde who had hailed him. There was something about her that was familiar. Maybe these women weren't prostitutes after all and she was an old acquaintance. Out of sheer curiosity he applied the brakes and drew up to the kerb. What was it about the girl that had touched his memory? Before he could work it out, the blonde was round at his window, peering at him.

'I'm going to Ormesby, love,' she said through lips layered with lipstick. She was already reaching for the back door handle.

'What about the others?' he said, watching the dark-haired girl in his mirror, struggling to place her, feeling there was something he should be remembering about her, the way, when he'd served in Northern Ireland, he'd developed a sixth sense for recalling dangerous faces from photographs.

By now the blonde had the door open and was hauling herself in.

'They live in different directions,' she said and slammed the door. 'Only one fare for you tonight, darling.' She giggled. 'But you got the fairest of the fares.'

'Fair enough,' Eddie said, playing along, his eyes still watching the dark-haired girl in the mirror as he pulled away, irritated that he couldn't place her.

Later on in the journey, still scratching at his memory, he asked the blonde about her.

'The dark-haired girl back there. I've seen her somewhere. Can't place her though.'

The woman snorted. 'Clara the snob. Lady Clara who wears a tiara. You wouldn't want to know her, pet.'

'A snob, is she?'

'Thinks she's a cut above, that one,' the blonde continued, warming to her theme. 'Got special clients and is very secretive about where she lives, like she's afraid we'll all turn up for tea and crumpets one afternoon when it doesn't suit.'

'Lady Muck, eh!' Eddie smiled at her in the mirror. The girl was still nagging at his memory. Except for her name and confirmation that she was a prostitute, the blonde in the back seat hadn't helped. But she wasn't finished yet.

'She's always going on about her daughter, is Clara. She's only six and the snotty little bitch has her at elec – electrocution lessons or something to make her speak proper. Pays for her to go to a private school over in Stockton as well.'

Clara was turning out to be something of an obsession with the blonde. Eddie let her ramble, punctuating her diatribes with occasional questions to gain more specific information. Yet, as they neared the blonde's destination, he still hadn't a clue as to why he thought Clara was familiar. Was it just a case of mistaken identity on his part?

When she was out of the cab the blonde paid up. Unabashed, she said, 'If you ever meet that Clara, don't tell her I said anything will you, darling? She's not that bad really.'

Amused by her sudden reversal, Eddie smiled, 'My lips are sealed, darling.'

Reassured, she flashed him a smile and tottered off into the night with an air of confidence about her, as though the inner woman was declaring to the world that, except for a quirk of fate, she would have been on the catwalks of the world. Eddie reflected, as he watched her disappear, that it must be her hard-edged confidence that enabled her to survive the night predators. Clara, the mystery woman, must be of the same ilk.

Half-way home, the warmth from the heater being languor-inducing, his mind comfortably in neutral, it came to him. The dark-haired girl's face floated up from his subconscious and he knew Clara was the girl in the photograph Alex had shown him, the girl who'd been part of the blackmail plot. It was too late to ring his pal now and tell him. He would do that tomorrow but what Alex would want to do about it, only heaven knew.

CHAPTER 20

Two days after Eddie had reported his sighting, Alex parked his car in the street outside Rose House private school. He was uncomfortable, worried that somebody might mistake him for a paedophile or something equally nasty, because that's the way it was these days if you hung around school entrances without good reason. Eddie's phone call informing him about the girl and telling him he'd understood she had a daughter at a private school in Stockton was his reason for being here.

He'd made up his mind that he wanted to hit back at Bridge, had a vague idea he'd force money out of the gangster to compensate Clark and his family. Eddie's call had given him a place to start; he had to stop brooding and take some action or he'd go crazy.

A cluster of mothers were gathered at the school gate but he couldn't see Clara. Perhaps Eddie had it wrong. This was definitely the only private school for young children in Stockton, but it was a bit of a gamble that Clara would pick up her child. She could easily have made other arrangements for her collection, another mother perhaps, or taking it in turns.

He was beginning to think his idea foolish, a product of his desperation, when he caught a movement in the distance, a female figure running. As she came into sharper focus the breeze blew her dark hair away from her face and he recognized the girl responsible for his entrapment. She looked so innocent as she blended in with the mothers, and Alex noticed she was smart and well-dressed. The others greeted her warmly enough and he had to admit she looked just like any one of them, no hint of that darker side, the side that had been prepared to ruin his life.

The first child charged out of the gates in wild abandon like a young colt released into pasture, ran straight to her mother. Then other young colts rampaged through the gates and ran to their parents. Through the open window Alex could hear high-pitched voices merging into an unintelligible cacophony. Not for the first time in his life, he wondered how teachers put up with it.

His eyes never left Clara. The memory of that portentous night in the pub returned now as he studied her. He felt anger and bitter resentment towards her for the way she had used him; he hadn't been a person at all to her, just a thing. The small blonde girl who ran up and threw her arms around her clearly wasn't viewed as a thing, a dispensable commodity. It was obvious from the way Clara's face lit up, the way she bent to kiss her forehead, that the child was dearly loved. Alex would have found the scene quite touching if he hadn't known what one of the participants was capable of.

Clara took the child's hand, led her along the pavement to a red Nissan Micra, put her daughter in the front passenger seat. Alex started his Mazda, followed when she moved off, careful to keep a safe distance so she wouldn't be suspicious.

Clara drove through built-up areas observing the speed limit. Alex kept so far back that he almost lost her at a set of traffic lights but managed to catch up again. Eventually they left the Stockton suburbs and travelled country roads towards the small town of Yarm.

Just when he was sure they were going right into Yarm itself the Micra made a turn into a housing estate that had crept out from the edges of the town towards the surrounding country-side. Alex slowed right down, concentrating hard to balance the need to keep her in sight against the risk of coming too close. To do that, more than once he allowed her out of his sight and, thinking he'd lost her, was relieved to catch her again.

When she eventually pulled on to a driveway he drove straight past, eyes straight ahead. After parking further up the road he watched mother and daughter get out and enter the house. He gave it a minute then drove back again, this time taking more notice of the house, which was semi-detached and expensive-looking, as were all the other houses he'd seen here. For sure, no one on a poor or even average income could afford them. Was there a husband? He doubted it somehow. What kind of man could condone her nefarious professional activities, unless she kept them secret from him or was a lowlife himself?

What was he going to do now? He decided, since he had no time to waste, that boldness would be best. Confronting Clara in her own home might just shake her enough to make her talk. If there was a man in her life, there was a good chance he'd still be at work and, though he didn't like the idea of her little girl being around, Clara would surely have enough sense to keep her out of the way while they talked.

His mind made up, he drove back, parked outside the house and walked up the drive. She was quick to answer his knocking. He watched the expression in her eyes pass through neutral to puzzlement, settle on fear as she realized where she had seen him before.

'Yes, it's me,' he said. 'In the flesh but with more clothes on than last time.'

Desperation flooded her eyes. She glanced over her shoulder, then back at Alex. Her instinct was telling her to slam the door and run but she knew she had the child to consider. Desperation gave way to weary resignation because there was no way to escape the man standing before her.

Alex allowed himself a small amount of satisfaction in watching her predicament. For what she'd done to him it was less than she deserved, but it wasn't going to help his cause.

'I just want to talk,' he said, trying to reassure her he wouldn't harm her. 'We can do it out here or inside.'

It didn't convince Clara. She shrank away from him and tried to shut the door. He blocked it with his foot, pushed it open again.

'No!' she cried. 'You're going to hurt me and I've got a kid in here.'

'I know that,' he said. 'I won't hurt you or the child if you co-operate.'

Unsure of him, she looked up and down the street, seeking refuge. But it was quiet, nobody about. He waited calmly until she decided there was no way out of it, that she'd have to trust him. Biting her top lip nervously, she capitulated and let him come in.

He followed her down the hallway into the living room. The whole décor was white: the wallpaper, the rug, the sofa and chairs. He wondered if it was a subconscious attempt to contrast her home with the dirty way she earned the money to furnish it. The little girl was sitting at a white piano in the corner of the room, tentatively poking at the keys. It was like a picture from a magazine, something to aspire to.

'Go up to your bedroom, please, Pauline. Mummy has a visitor.'

Obediently, the girl climbed off the stool and crossed the room to the door. As she passed she smiled sweetly at Alex and, momentarily, he saw the mother's face, as it once had been, in her face. It made him sad.

'Sweet child,' he commented, then bitterly: 'Pity about the mother, though. Clara's the name, isn't it?'

She nodded and lit a cigarette. Alex noticed her hand was shaking.

As a cloud of smoke drifted away, she asked, 'How did you find me?'

'Irrelevant!' He could hear the vestigial anger in his own voice.

'What is it you want?' she asked, trembling.

'I want the name of the guy who set it up. Was it the fat guy?'

Clara blenched, made an effort to control herself. 'Look, it was nothing personal. I'm sorry.'

His anger resurged. 'Everything's personal and you're evading me.'

Her hand started to shake again. A piece of ash fell on to the carpet.

'You don't understand. He'll kill me if I talk. He'll kill you too.'

Alex sighed. He could see Clara was genuinely frightened but he'd have to put more pressure on.

'If I don't get an answer I'm going to make it known, to all and sundry in that posh school your daughter attends, just what one of their parents' professional activity entails. Then, as a bonus, I'll make sure your neighbours get to know.'

He had no intention of carrying out his threat, couldn't do that to the child. Watching Clara's consternation, though, he knew she was imagining the collapse of the little world she had built for herself and her precious daughter. But she had brought this on herself and he was on a mission. Reluctantly, but determined to see this through, he turned the screw further.

'I've a friend who took photographs of your nocturnal wanderings,' he lied. 'You might say it's case of the biter bit because I'm willing to send them out.'

That seemed to hit home. More ash fell on to the carpet. She stamped on it with her foot, disposed of the cigarette in an ashtray. Then the tears came and she covered her face with her hands.

'He'll kill me!' she groaned. 'He'll kill me.'

Alex, his tone softening, said, 'Nobody will know I got it from you. You've a lovely little girl upstairs and I'm not a man who would let anything happen to her mother, even though that mother has harmed me. But I do need information and I will expose you if you withhold it.'

Her hands dropped away from her eyes which were glistening with tears. She was wondering whether she dared trust him.

At last she spoke. 'You'll keep me out of it? You promise?'

'I'm a doctor. This dirty work has been forced on me but I still value life, yours included. Believe me, I'll keep my word.'

Biting her fingernails, she stared at the far corner of the room while he waited patiently. He thought she was going to shut him out again, that her fear was going to preclude any other emotion or impulse. Then, suddenly, she turned her gaze back to him.

'The one with me that night. His name is Grimes, Jack Grimes.'

'A dirty name if ever I heard one. Rhymes with crimes. Where does he live?'

She didn't hesitate. 'Great Ayton, 14 Hollywell Road.'

'Nice little village that,' Alex mused. 'What is he to you, Clara?'

'Nothing at all. Sometimes he sets me up with rich clients. That's all.'

Alex lowered his head, looked at her from under his eyebrows and pushed the boat out.

'That night you and he were working for Charles Bridge. Did you know that?'

Alex noticed her sharp intake of breath. Bridge's name had an effect on her, no doubt about that.

'Grimes bragged about working for him, said he was big time. But that night I didn't know who he was working for. I swear it. All I was interested in was the money he paid me.'

'The root of all evil.'

Whether it was from anger or shame, he didn't know but Clara's face went red.

'I'm a single mother. Money keeps my daughter in a good school, gives her chances I never had. There are no druggies on the streets round here. Wouldn't you do something for your daughter if you were me?'

Her attempt at self-justification annoyed him. 'Bridge threatened my daughter, my family. How would you like it if your daughter were threatened by a gangster like him? You were part of it, lady, for the sake of dirty money.'

He hadn't intended to launch an attack but he saw it had hit home. Clara lowered her head, couldn't meet his eye.

'Grimes told me none of that. He just said they were setting you up for your wife.'

'He lied, of course. It was to put pressure on me to help Bridge escape from prison. That's what you were part of, Clara. Small ripples become dangerous waves, don't they?'

She couldn't answer him. Alex decided it was time to go. He rose and started across the room. Clara remained seated but called out to him, her voice hoarse.

'There's more. It might help you.'

He halted mid-stride, went back, sat on the edge of the chair and leaned towards her. She was biting her nails. He figured she was still afraid but, somehow, he had disturbed her conscience.

'Fire away,' he said. 'I'm all ears.'

'Sometimes I clean Grimes's house for him,' she began. 'He lives on his own and pays me for it. One day I found something in the bin, part of a letter he'd torn up. But he hadn't done it well enough because I could still get the gist and it disturbed me.'

She hesitated, eyes far away, face drawn, as though at a dark place in her mind she was staring down into a precipice with one foot raised tentatively, knowing that there could be no going back once she took the next step. Alex waited patiently for her to commit herself.

It came out in a rush, like water from a broken dam. 'The letter was from the hospital telling Grimes he'd tested positive for Aids, that he had to report for treatment.'

Alex blew out his cheeks. Her announcement had been certainly dramatic. But was it any use to him? As he pondered the matter she raised her head and looked straight at him. She was clearly relieved, as though she'd carried a secret too long, was glad now she'd shared it with someone and wanted to say more.

He met her gaze and rubbed his chin thoughtfully. 'Why do I get the feeling there's more to tell?'

The whole dam collapsed and it came gushing out in a torrent. 'There was a girl living with Grimes, only sixteen years old. She left him and later wrote to me telling me she had the virus. She said it must have been Grimes because he was the only one she'd been with. She wouldn't tell her family or anyone it was him because she was afraid he'd hurt them.'

Alex shook his head sadly. 'So young and so naïve.'

Clara glared at him. 'She paid the price for her naïvety. She died! Then her parents wrote to me because they found one of my letters to her. They couldn't understand why she hadn't spoken out. They thought I might know something.'

Alex grimaced. 'It was tantamount to murder. I take it you didn't tell the parents the truth.'

A single tear rolled down her cheek, dropped on to the white carpet.

'I wanted to but I was afraid he would harm me or my daughter if he found out. I've been feeling bad about it.'

Another tear started its journey. 'If Grimes finds out I told you all this I'm dead.'

'He won't know,' Alex reassured her.

'Someone has to stop him.' She was mumbling so that he hardly heard. 'Maybe it was providence brought you here.'

For a moment, he was bemused. 'Stop him! You mean he's still at it.' Then, surprised at his own naïvety, he added quietly. 'So there have been others?'

Clara hissed, 'Of course there have?'

After that there didn't seem much more to say. The magnitude of Grimes's evil seemed to hang between them, a sinister force to take the breath away. Alex stood, stared down at Clara, pitying her sad life and the sad company she kept, wishing he'd never laid eyes on her.

'I'll be paying Mr Grimes a visit.'

'You'll stop him doing it again?'

'I'll certainly frighten him.'

'And you'll keep me out of it? You promise?'

'That's what I said.'

Clara followed him to the door. As he opened it, he glanced up, noticed the daughter sitting on the stairs watching them. She smiled and waved at him.

He said, 'Hope she never finds out.'

Clara's brow wrinkled. She looked at her daughter. 'Finds out what?'

'How much it's costing your soul keeping her in that nice school.'

She glared at Alex, who knew he'd touched a nerve. 'Look to your own soul! I've a feeling it's been in bad trouble and there's more coming its way.'

He smiled ruefully. 'Nothing's more certain,' he said. 'Nothing's more certain.'

CHAPTER 21

Number 14 Holywell Road, Great Ayton, the abode of Jack Grimes, purveyor of death by disease, could easily have been the home of a country gent. Even in the dark, studying it through the slits of his balaclava, Alex could see that. He was at the back of the detached house where the extensive garden, thick with trees and shrubbery, would offer enough cover for his approach.

He slipped inside the back gate, crossed the lawn and flattened himself against the wall. After a minute waiting there, he decided it was safe to move and edged towards the nearest window. It was open half an inch. Grimes must be a confident man to leave it like that these days, or maybe he felt his reputation was enough security. Either way, it was no problem for Alex to raise it and scramble in.

A shaft of moonlight gave him enough light to see he had entered the kitchen. Avoiding tables and chairs, he crossed the room and entered the long hall. He paused and listened. Like a giant heartbeat for the whole house, the grandfather clock's ticking dominated. He heard other sounds further off, a raucous rise and a sibilant falling away and realized someone was snoring upstairs.

He climbed the stairs. One of the bedrooms was the source of the noise. The door was open slightly and the snoring was sonorous now, like being close to an animal in its lair. He thought of Grimes like that, an atavistic force in his primitive cave. This was a point of no return and he hesitated, knowing once he stepped inside that room he was committed. Part of him was reluctant, so he had to steel his resolve before he slipped inside the door.

It was darker in the bedroom. Alex stood still allowing his eyes to adjust. He could make out Grimes on the bed; he was lying on his back, chest rising and falling, each descent accompanied by a whistling sound which, in any other circumstances, might have been comical. Alex felt inside his pocket for the syringe, reached into another pocket for the handcuffs. Eyes fixed on Grimes's supine figure, he approached the bed.

Not allowing himself a moment's hesitation, he grabbed one of Grimes's wrists, slipped a handcuff on, then locked the other one around one of the metal rods at the head of the bed. Grimes woke with a start. As he thrashed about like an animal caught in a snare and let go a string of imprecations, Alex stepped back. Content that this man was exactly as he wanted him, he switched on the bedside light.

Grimes looked up, his eyes mere slits as they adjusted. Sweat beads were forming on his bald head. One rivulet of perspiration ran down his temple, under his eye and on to his cheek. His corpulent frame was on its side, the restrained arm above his head, the other flapping in frustration at the bedclothes like a beached walrus in a temper.

Alex spoke first, kept his voice clear and level. 'There's an easy way to get out of your current predicament. You just have to tell me right now where I can find Charles Bridge. That will do it.'

Behind Grimes's eyes, Alex could see wheels turning, calculations being made.

'How should I know where he is?'

'You should. You work for him. Pity for you if you don't know.'

Grimes frowned. 'What do you mean?' he grunted, lip curling.

Wordlessly, Alex reached inside his pocket and brought out a phial filled with red liquid. He placed it on the bed cabinet out of Grimes's reach. Next, he took a syringe from the same pocket. With slow deliberation, he filled the syringe. Grimes watched him with wide eyes.

'It's blood,' Alex said, putting the bottle back in his pocket and then holding the syringe under the bedside light. 'We can't do without it, can we? Only it has to be uncorrupted. But therein lies the rub, eh Jack!'

Grimes fixed his gaze on the syringe. Alex watched him working it out, could see Grimes didn't want to go to the conclusion where his mind was leading him.

'What are you talking about?' he said, voice desiccated.

Alex brandished the syringe. 'Like you, Jack, this blood is corrupted. It contains the aids virus. Now, that is something you'll be familiar with.'

Grimes shrank away from the syringe, shifted his position on the bed so he was as far from it as he could be, given the restraint imposed by the handcuffs. Pure hatred emanated from his eyes as he stared at Alex.

'I don't know what you're talking about,' he snapped, a tremor in his voice.

Alex sighed. 'If I add this to your own blood, it won't do you much good, will it? Could be a lethal cocktail, seeing as you're already infected.'

Grimes's eyes bulged. His fear was unbridled. Alex had thrust a spear into a secret and vulnerable place. In frustration, he yanked at the handcuffs but to no avail.

Spent, he turned his attention back to his tormentor, snarled. 'How do you know?'

'That doesn't matter. All you need focus on is that I'm going to stick you with this needle if I don't get what I want. Now do yourself a favour, man, and tell me where Bridge is.'

'No way! He'll kill me!'

'I won't be telling him it came from you, so don't concern yourself about that.'

A silence developed, Grimes considering his dilemma. Alex decided he needed another push and raised the syringe.

'Pity about this. It's a nasty way to go, don't you think?'

Grimes made up his mind, held up his free hand as though he was stopping traffic coming at him too fast for comfort.

'He's in Saltburn, Runswick Street, number twelve.'

'You'd better not be lying. I've got too much on you, matey, enough to turn your world black.'

'It's the truth,' Grimes protested. 'Just you keep your mouth shut about where it came from.'

Alex didn't answer him. He raised the syringe, moved it in Grimes's direction. The criminal shrank away, mouth opening in horror. His hand rose in an effort to protect himself. Alex squirted the syringe under his guard. The red liquid hit his face, diffused and ran down his cheeks. In a panic, Grimes wiped it away and stared at the residue on his hand.

'A waste of good red wine, wasn't it?' Alex said, without the least compassion.

Grimes wiped his mouth with the back of his free hand, tasted the liquid. Relief that it was indeed wine gave way to anger. He stared at Alex, eyes narrowed down to slits.

'If I find out who you are and who told you I'll—'

'You won't be doing anything,' Alex interrupted. 'If anything violent happens to me there's a letter with my solicitor. It'll be sent to the medical authorities informing them how you've been spreading the virus, how one of your victims died. It even names her. They'll call it murder, won't they?'

Grimes was crestfallen, didn't know what to say. Alex had

him trapped with no room to manoeuvre and he knew it. His lips started to work but he couldn't find words and he floundered.

'Dumbstruck suits you,' Alex told him. 'Pity there isn't a little more shame involved, though.'

'Bridge will kill you,' Grimes said, 'and I'll spit on your grave.'

'Will you, now,' Alex retorted, 'because if it happens that way the letter will wing its way to the authorities. Ask me, Grimes, you should be praying that I outlive you.'

Grimes shut his mouth. With a sigh of exasperation, he sank back on the pillow and stared at the ceiling. Usually, by false charm or bullying, he could find his way around a problem, but there was no solution to this one.

Alex felt a certain satisfaction because he'd struck a blow at those who'd used and abused him and it made him feel better. Satisfied with his night's work so far, he placed the key to the handcuffs on the cabinet just out of reach of Grimes's free hand.

'By the time your pea brain is inventive enough to find a way of reaching that key, I'll be long gone,' he informed Grimes. 'Don't forget, if I find out that you let Bridge know I'm coming, there's still that letter. Besides, I don't think Bridge will be too happy you talked, do you?'

With that final warning he walked out of the room. He left the same way he'd entered, removing his balaclava before he was on the street. A quick call on his mobile told Eddie, who had dropped him and was cruising the area in his taxi, where to pick him up.

'Mission accomplished?' Eddie queried as Alex climbed into the cab.

'He squealed like the pig he is.'

'So you know where the boss man is hiding out?'

'I know,' Alex said. 'Tomorrow night I'll pay him a visit and relieve him of some of his money.'

'You sure you know what you're doing?'

'The money is for the injured prison officer and his family.'

'I know that. How do you feel now?'

'Better than I've been. At least I'm hitting back.'

Eddie gave him a worried look. 'The best plans can go wrong, you know?'

'Don't worry, he won't know who I am when I go in with that balaclava on. Grimes didn't have a clue. Will you take me there, Eddie?'

'You don't have to ask. You've backed me up enough times.'

Alex smiled. He was grateful he had a friend like Eddie and couldn't put a price on the friendship they'd forged in mutual hardship and danger. He was sure he wouldn't need him to do anything more than drive and didn't want to put him in danger but, on the off chance that something went wrong, he couldn't wish for a better man behind him.

CHAPTER 22

Alex spent the next day alone in Eddie's flat. It dragged by like the times he'd been on guard duty in the army. He felt he could have happily excised it from the number of his days, except that subconsciously he was psyching himself up for a confrontation with Charles Bridge. Eddie came back late in the afternoon with the shotgun he'd procured from one of the disreputable characters with whom he came into contact on the streets during his driving jobs. The guy apparently owed him a favour.

That night Eddie took his car instead of his taxi. They parked fifty yards down the road from number 12 Runswick Street, Saltburn, the temporary domicile of one Charles Bridge. It was a typical suburban, semi-detached house, a place you'd hardly expect to serve as a sanctuary for a criminal on the run, though maybe its very ordinariness meant nobody would suspect. They watched the house for ten minutes, saw nothing out of the ordinary and were conscious that the locals might suspect they were the ones up to no good if they sat there too long.

'Pass it over,' Alex said. 'Might as well get it done.'

Eddie reached under the driver's seat, passed the shotgun over. Alex could tell from the look on his face he was worried.

'You're going in blind,' Eddie muttered. 'You don't know how many are in there. Maybe I should come with you.'

'You're doing enough,' Alex told him. 'Right now, I'm confident I can do it alone.'

Eddie shook his head. 'Don't be too confident. You're not a soldier any more. Are you doing the right thing? Think about it, Alex. Too much has happened to you. Maybe you're not thinking straight. You could always call the police, let them deal with Bridge.'

'Afterwards,' Alex grunted. 'First I get money out of him for the injured officer, then we'll call the police.'

'Something could go wrong,' Eddie said, staring straight ahead as though the future would reveal itself on the windscreen if he stared hard enough. 'You might have to pull the trigger and then your life is finished. Think about Ann. What would that do to her?'

Alex didn't answer. Eddie gave a long sigh, swivelled his eyes to face him straight on. Alex opened the barrel of the shotgun and ejected the cartridges. Holding them in his palm, he handed them to his pal.

'Now I won't be able to shoot anybody.'

Eddie shook his head ruefully. 'Catch 22. Now if he calls your bluff, you'll be the one dead.'

'I'll take him by surprise, like I did Grimes. He won't get the chance to shoot me.'

'Rambo hasn't got anything on you, has he?' Eddie groaned. But he knew there was no use arguing. Alex's mind was made up and he wasn't going to alter it. Reluctantly, Eddie accepted that all he could do was back him up.

'I'll wait here,' he continued. 'Soon as it's done we're out of here. Then we'll call the police. That bastard needs to be back behind bars.'

'Of course,' Alex said. He opened the long black coat Eddie had lent him, hid the shotgun in the folds and reached for the door. Before he had a foot on the pavement, Eddie put a hand on his shoulder and hauled him back in.

149

'I'm not changing my mind,' Alex said, a trace of annoyance in his voice.

Eddie pointed up the street. 'Look! The door's opened. Someone's leaving the house.'

They watched a blond-haired woman step out of the front door. In the semi-darkness it was difficult to see her features clearly as she hesitated at the gate and looked up and down the street. Seemingly satisfied, she closed the door behind her, walked briskly down the path and climbed into the Ford Fiesta parked at the kerb.

Alex said, 'I read his record. His only relative is a sister. That could be her or a girlfriend. Likely he'll be alone now.'

'You mean, hopefully, he will,' Eddie rejoined. 'You don't know for sure.'

The Fiesta's lights came on and it started moving towards them. Both men sank right down in their seats and waited until the headlights had swept over them before they sat back up.

'If anything kicks off just get out of here,' Alex warned. 'I don't want you held responsible for anything. You dropped me off and that was all. Right?'

Eddie didn't answer, just watched Alex climb out of the car. Alex put a flat cap on his head and with the weapon under his coat again, set off in the direction of the house.

He didn't break his stride, just kept his head down against the blustery wind as he walked past the house to the other end of the street where he made a right turn, then a sharp right. That brought him into the narrow lane they'd reconnoitred earlier which ran behind the houses. Apart from a solitary dog heading straight for him which at the last minute decided to walk around him in a wide arc, he didn't meet another soul. Lights shone from bedroom windows and he figured that at this time of night folk would be preparing for bed.

It was easy work to step over the low fence and make his way down the narrow passage between two garages. They'd spotted its potential earlier and it meant he could approach the target house without being visible. He could see there were no lights at the back of the house. Better still, his position was only a few yards from the back door.

Wedged in the passageway, he leaned back and gathered his nerve. For him this was not an unfamiliar scenario. He'd been in similar positions countless times during his army service. The main difference on this occasion was that he was entirely alone, no one to think about but himself and his enemy. He could feel his breathing accelerate. As his mind sent out its messages, the adrenalin surged through his veins in response. Sucking in lungfuls of air to calm himself, he counted to three, then burst from his cover, the shotgun against his chest.

He spun at the last second to let his back take the impact as he crashed against the wall. For a minute, he held his position, watching and listening for any sign that he might have been seen by a neighbour or maybe someone inside. The only sounds were those made by the wind as it groaned between the garages and rattled a loose fence.

He rested the shotgun on the ground, pulled on his balaclava, stripped off his coat and picked the weapon up again. He held the coat against the back door, covering the glass panelling. Then he drove the shotgun hard into the glass, which gave on the first impact, the sound muffled by the material. Hoping the key would be in the lock, he reached a hand through the hole, was relieved when he felt the cold metal protuberance on the other side. One turn and the lock opened.

He slipped on his coat, went down on his haunches. Gripping the shotgun tightly in one hand, he turned the door handle with the other, pushed the door open, rolled inside the kitchen, ended up on his back with the shotgun on his chest.

He lay there, listening, while his eyes adjusted to the

surroundings. Satisfied that nobody had heard him enter, he stood up and crossed to the kitchen door. It led into the hallway. A shaft of light from a door at the other end of the hall created a rectangular pattern on the carpet.

Shotgun held out in front of him, he tiptoed down the hall. Readying himself, he poked his head through the door and saw Bridge sitting in front of a gas fire, a newspaper on his lap.

Alex stepped inside the room. Something, perhaps a sixth sense, caused the criminal to lift his head. He stared straight at Alex. Shock registered on his face. He let go of the newspaper and it fell on to the floor. Alex saw that his beard was longer now but the hint of arrogance was still there in the eyes, even as they bulged with fear.

With swift strides Alex crossed the room. His gaze never leaving Bridge for a moment, he turned the television off. The gangster was sitting upright, his body rigid, mesmerized by the shotgun, not sure whether at any second it would blast him into eternity. Alex allowed the silence to stimulate Bridge's doubt and trepidation even further, enjoying the fact that the tables were turned on the man who'd had no qualms about ruining him.

It was Bridge who broke the silence, a slight quiver in his voice. 'What is it you want?'

Alex put on the guttural Glaswegian accent assimilated at his grandmother's knee, refined in later life when his battalion had been posted to the same town as the local Glaswegian regiment. He hoped it would be good enough to deceive the gangster.

'I'm wanting your money, pal.' he grunted. 'Money or your life, like the highwaymen used to say.'

Bridge's eyes narrowed. 'You know who I am, do you?'

'I ken all right.'

'Who sent you?'

'I'm ma own man. Nobody sent me. Where'd you keep it?'

The gangster's lower lip protruded. Alex could see his duplicitous mind was at work, trying to find a way through this situation, wondering if there was a way to turn it around.

'You were badly advised. I haven't much money.'

Alex stepped towards him, lifted the shotgun. Bridge stared down the barrels, hypnotized as they stopped inches away from his face.

'Charlie Bridge is'nae a poor man and I'm no a patient one. You're going to give me money or I'm going to blast you. You'll no be missed, either. There's people will thank me for it.'

Bridge managed to haul his eyes away from the barrels up to the masked face. Hatred and malice emanated from him. Alex felt the full force of the man's evil, an evil thwarted, struggling to accept the loss of power on which it thrived.

'How do you know me? How did you know I was here?'

Alex answer was to push the barrels right against the centre of his forehead. He was sweating under the balaclava, aware that the shotgun was an empty threat, that if Bridge decided to be brave, he'd be in trouble.

'You were seen, the first day you came here,' Alex lied. 'One of the cons who knew you in prison recognized your ugly puss. He was too scared to turn you in but to a desperate man with a habit, you're heaven sent.'

'You're desperate because you've got a habit?'

'Who has'nae a habit? A man like you has money to fix it, so cough it up.'

A frown creased Bridge's forehead. Alex liked the way the conversation had developed because the gangster obviously understood a man in need of drugs would sometimes do anything for cash. Worse, if such a man didn't get what he wanted, his behaviour could be unpredictable.

'OK! OK!' Bridge exclaimed, raising his hands in a gesture of surrender. 'The money's in the cupboard under the stairs. Now get that shotgun out of my face.'

Alex took two steps backwards. He gestured towards the door with his weapon.

'Be a good wee boy, Charlie, and go and get it for me.'

Bridge stood up, sucked in his cheeks, resentment written in his features and body movements. Taking a wide arc to keep away from the shotgun, he crossed the room. Alex followed behind him as he stepped into the hall and pushed a light-switch.

'In there,' Bridge grunted. He pointed to a small cupboard no more than two feet high under the stair. 'It's in a suitcase.'

'So do the honours.'

Bridge got down, opened the cupboard, reached in as far as his arm would go and hauled out a brown suitcase. He glared up at Alex.

'Open it,' Alex commanded. 'But be very careful about it.'

Still on his knees, Bridge undid the clasps. Alex was thinking that so far this had been easy, perhaps too easy. It proved no idle presentiment. Bridge opened the case, reached in and his hand emerged holding a gun. The barrel started to rise.

In a reflex action, Alex kicked out, connected with the gangster's wrist, diverted his aim. He followed that up with a swipe at the gangster's head with the shotgun barrel, heard him groan as the steel impacted on his jaw. The blow knocked Bridge off balance. He toppled, sprawled on the floor but survival instinct made him hold on to the gun. Without giving him a chance to use it Alex loomed over him and stamped down on his hand. Yelling in pain, he released his grip and Alex kicked the weapon away. Covering Bridge with the shotgun, he bent down, picked it up and slid it into his pocket.

For a moment the only sound was the two men breathing hard. Bridge was still on the floor, holding his jaw with his undamaged hand. Alex was staring down at him, his nearness to death a moment ago sinking in now. But he wasn't going to let the gangster know how shaken he was.

'Warned you,' he said. He hauled the suitcase away from Bridge, noticing the gangster's jaw was swelling.

Bridge watched helplessly as Alex opened the suitcase himself. When he saw it was full of money, he gave a low whistle.

'Small change to you,' he said, glancing at Bridge as he closed the case. 'But it'll do for me.'

Bridge was holding his jaw and looking at his bruised fingers.

'I'll find out what hole you crawled out of,' he moaned, spitting a cascade of blood and teeth on to the carpet.

'There's nae chance of that,' Alex told him. 'It's a far cry to Scotland and I'll be amongst my own there.'

The shotgun in one hand, the suitcase in the other, he backed down the hallway to the front door. Bridge just watched from the floor. At the end of the hallway Alex paused and called out to him.

'Stay where you are. Stick your head out and I'll blow that jaw away altogether.'

He stepped outside, removed the balaclava, hid the shotgun under his coat and walked briskly down the street. Half-away back, a car passed him, its headlights catching him in their glare. He lowered his head as a precaution but wasn't unduly worried.

Eddie saw him coming, drove towards him. He tumbled into the passenger seat, put the shotgun on the floor while Eddie executed a three-point turn and shot off the way he had come.

When they were well clear Eddie glanced at the suitcase on his friend's knee.

'Mission accomplished?'

Still breathing hard, Alex tapped the suitcase. 'There's plenty in here for the officer and his family.'

'No trouble in there?'

'Sure there was. Bridge tried it on but I gave him a battering.'

'For God's sake, you didn't kill him?'

'You know me better than that.'

Relieved, Eddie smiled. 'So when do I call the police?'

'Soon as you can pull in.'

A moment passed. Eddie said, 'Did you see a car back there?'

'A car passed me. What about it?'

'You had your balaclava off?'

'Thought it best to take it off in the street.'

Eddie grimaced, 'I think it was the blonde woman coming back.'

Alex thought about it. 'If it was, she wouldn't know me and in any case the police will arrest her too.'

'Of course. Just thought I'd mention it.'

Alex pointed to a parade of shops off to the left where there were two telephone booths.

'Park out of sight and make the call there will you, old son? Then we can go home and relax.'

Eddie drove past, pulled into a pub car park. He got out and walked back.

Alone in the car, Alex felt exhausted. Most of the tension had drained away and reaction had set in. When Bridge had pointed the gun back there, he'd thought he was a dead man. But he'd pulled it off, emerged unscathed.

'It's done and dusted,' Eddie declared as he climbed back in the car a few minutes later. 'You look exhausted, though. Stay at my place tonight if you want.'

'Appreciate the offer but I'll collect my car and drive back. I'd better hide the money out there in the country near my place.' He paused. 'Thanks for your help by the way. Gave me confidence having you along.'

Eddie smiled. 'Let's just say it was our last hurrah.'

'I'll drink to that.'

CHAPTER 23

Late that same night, back at the old farmhouse, Alex lay back in his chair, supped his whisky and stared at the wads of money scattered on the coffee table in front of him. It totalled £60,000, an amount which, he had no doubt, would represent no more than pocket money to Bridge. But it could do a great deal for Officer Clark's family. The problem would be how to pass it over without too much fuss, without the family knowing its source. A gift from a mysterious sympathizer might do it. Right now, at two in the morning, he didn't want to think too much about the detail.

He put his head back, listened to the dreamy, late-night music from the radio. He was tuned to a local station, had heard a couple of news bulletins in the last hour but nothing about Bridge being arrested. That didn't worry him unduly; maybe the police hadn't released the information, were saving it for a press conference in the morning. But he would feel better when he knew Bridge was recaptured and off the streets. That was his last thought as fatigue overcame him and he drifted off to sleep in his chair.

The ringing in his head irritated him, wouldn't go away, seemed to be coming from a long way off. He opened his eyes, realized it was the telephone ambushing his sleep. He glanced at his watch; it was half-past two. Who could be calling at this time of night? He could only think of Eddie, maybe checking up on him. Who else at this unearthly hour? Perhaps his old pal had news about Bridge's arrest.

'Enjoy your evening out, did you, Mac?'

It wasn't Eddie's voice and, still half-asleep, he had difficulty recognizing its owner. A wrong number probably, though there was something familiar.

'Who is this?'

'What happened to the Scottish accent? Lose it somewhere on the moors, did you?'

A bitter taste gathered in Alex's mouth. He hadn't recognized the voice because it must have been distorted by missing teeth and a swollen jaw. But, with a sinking feeling, he knew it belonged to Bridge, that he must have escaped the police. Like water being dragged down a plughole, he felt himself spiralling back into that black abyss from which he'd struggled to emerge.

'Struck dumb, are you?'

Alex had to dig deep for composure, managed to squeeze out his words.

'What do you want?'

'Stupid question. But then you've been stupid. Have to admit I had a bit of luck, though. My sister came back and got me out of there in the nick of time. Calling the police didn't work, Alex, so where does that leave you?'

His desperation growing with every word that emerged from Bridge's mouth, Alex wondered how the gangster could possibly know it had been he who had robbed him. How the sister had known he was about to be arrested was equally confusing? Alex tried to wriggle.

'I don't know what—'

The gangster cut him short. 'Don't waste your breath. I want my money back.'

Alex fell silent. Nothing he could say was going to make any difference. For all he knew, Bridge could be just down the road with his henchmen, ready to storm the place. Head on the block, expecting the axe to fall at any minute, he waited tensely. Bridge delivered the blow with his next announcement.

'Remember what I said about your family? What I would do. Well – I did it.'

Alex's nerves screamed. He bit hard on his lip. He hardly dared ask the question.

'What have you done? If you've—'

Bridge's laughter echoed down the phone, mocking him. Thoughts raced through Alex's mind, each one flaying him with increasing force. He cursed himself for believing he could best the gangster without risking the safety of those dearest to him. Madness must have descended upon him. How would he live with himself if anything had happened to Liz and Ann? He'd surely messed up again. Was there no limit to his ego?

'Don't worry,' Bridge sneered. 'I didn't kill them but only because you're going to give me my money back in exchange for their lives.'

'If you hurt one hair on their heads, I'll—'

'Sure you will,' Bridge interrupted. 'But getting back to business, you're going to do exactly what I say. Then you'll get your darlings back in one piece.'

Alex forced back his anger. 'What do you want me to do?'

'It ain't difficult. You just have to be at the northbound side of the Washington service station midnight tomorrow, with my money. Wait in the car park. Make sure you have your mobile with you because you'll receive more instructions.'

Gripping the phone hard, Alex ran it through his head. He would have to do what he was told. Straightforward as the arrangement sounded, knowing Bridge there was sure to be a sting in the tail. He'd hurt the man's pride, hurt him physically. Bridge's ego wouldn't let that go.

He grunted into the mouthpiece. 'Midnight tomorrow, Washington services.'

'You've got it and this time no police. I'll know if they're around and it'll be your darlings who'll suffer.'

'There'll be nowhere in the world for you to hide if you hurt them.'

'So we understand each other?'

'We understand each other. You bring my family. I bring the money.'

Bridge sighed theatrically. 'All this trouble. My jaw is hurting and my fingers are throbbing and it's all for nothing. You might have known you couldn't beat me. I've had you fenced in from the start. That's how I do things.'

Alex couldn't resist asking. 'How did you know it was me who took the money?'

Bridge chuckled, ignored the question. 'What puzzles me is how you knew where I was?'

Alex mumbled, 'A lucky break.'

'Not so lucky now, then.'

Before Alex could say anything, Bridge hung up. Shaking with fear and anger, Alex put his phone on the cradle.

He didn't move for an hour, besieged by fears for Liz and Ann, and troubled in his conscience, because his attempts to boost his damaged ego had placed them in danger again. How had Bridge known it was him? It couldn't have been Jack Grimes. The man had been too frightened, surely, and Bridge had asked how he knew where he was, so Grimes couldn't have reported his visit. Nobody knew him in the area and the only person who could have seen him, and very briefly at that, was Bridge's sister in her car headlights. Yet, according to the gangster, she was the one who'd warned him he was about to be arrested. It seemed all to point to her but, against that, she didn't know him, did she? So how could she have recognized him last night and told her brother it was he who'd stolen his money? In the end he gave up trying to figure it out and hauled himself to bed.

Later, lying on top of the bedclothes, unable to sleep, he thought about tomorrow's meeting at the service station. If he was lucky it would be a straightforward exchange. But he didn't trust Bridge an inch. Regaining his money would hardly satisfy his vindictive streak. Alex decided that, rather than going into the situation blind, he'd have to ask Eddie to go with him to back him up. His friend would have to remain invisible but he would feel safer if he was there, armed and covering him.

CHAPTER 24

'Here we go again,' Eddie said, climbing into Alex's car and placing the shotgun under the seat. 'This is becoming a habit. Good job I didn't give the weapon back yet.'

They were outside Eddie's flat. He was referring to their trip up the motorway earlier that day to take a look at Washington Services and its environs so they wouldn't be going into the situation totally blind when Alex met Bridge.

'This time it could get dodgy,' Alex said. He looked worried. 'I don't like dragging you into this, mate, but I feel better you're with me.'

'We'll be a match for them,' Eddie replied. 'Two old soldiers like us.'

Alex wished he was that confident. They'd made a rough and ready plan but so much depended on Bridge's instructions when he rang Alex's mobile. He wondered if the fact that it was a clear night, the moon almost full, might help.

Alex drove along minor roads to the Al, then north towards Newcastle. It was an hour off midnight and the road was quiet enough. To be sure they weren't being followed he took a couple of minor detours off the motorway, then swung back on again.

Neither man was saying much; each was preparing himself mentally for what lay ahead. Alex forced himself to dismiss negative thoughts centring on his feeling that he was to blame for this mess, responsible for endangering his family and now his friend, because if he dwelled on them he wouldn't be in a fit state to deal with Bridge.

A hundred yards before the turn off for the service station Alex pulled off the motorway into a small parking area with a grassy embankment at the side. Eddie picked up the shotgun and opened the passenger door. A couple of cars went past, then there was a break in the traffic.

'I'll be somewhere near, even if you can't see me,' Eddie said.

'Good luck,' Alex told him, his face set.

Eddie put his thumb up and got out. Alex watched him scarper up the grassy incline and disappear over the top, before he pulled back on to the road.

A hundred yards further on he took the slip road which led into the Washington services. He drove past the cafeteria into the spacious car park. There were only a few cars but he parked well clear of them.

One of the parked cars was Eddie's, left there on their earlier visit that day. He'd crossed the bridge to the services on the south side of the motorway where Alex had picked him up in his car. The idea was, if Bridge changed the venue Eddie would follow Alex. It was a contingency plan of course, which neither Eddie nor he thought would be necessary. The fact that Bridge had brought them all the way up here seemed to indicate that this would be where the exchange would take place. How that would be done was the big question.

Alex cut the engine and studied his surroundings once more. The bridge spanning the motorway was glass-sided. Looking up from either car park, it was possible to see anyone crossing. The cafeteria was fifty yards from where he'd parked. Through the well-lit windows he could see the place was empty, except for a few stragglers, looking lonely hunched over their late night meals. Indeed, the place had the feel of a transit camp where lives intersected briefly before journeying again to who knew where. Where would Eddie take up his position? There were plenty of dark corners in the car park to lie up but Alex couldn't see him, which was how it should be. Suffice, if this business turned nasty, that he was there to help.

He glanced at his watch. Still twenty minutes to midnight. Was Bridge out there somewhere watching, counting down the minutes like an executioner? Though he didn't want it to, Alex's mind drifted back to all the events that had led to this critical moment in his life. His main aim, after he'd left the army, was to do something positive; becoming a doctor had fulfilled that need. Now, his life had gone into reverse; he was being forced into violent ways to save his family, the antithesis of the peaceful way he'd hoped to follow. That seemed perverse, no rhyme or reason.

The phone ringing drove away the mood, the encircling demons brought him back to the present with a jolt. He put it to his ear.

'Is that you, Bridge?'

'You were expecting someone else were you, Alex?'

'No! Right now you've got my full attention.'

'Good to hear I've got my teeth into you.'

Alex sighed. 'I'm where I should be. Where are you?'

'Not your concern. All you have to do is follow instructions to the letter and then we might all get away to our beds. You've got my money I presume?'

'Yes, so let's get on with it.'

'That's my boy. You see the bridge over the motorway?'

'Of course.'

'Bring the money across in the suitcase. Half-way, put the case down. There won't be anyone crossing but, if there is, wait till they're off the bridge and it's quiet. Then walk back to your end.'

'Just like that,' Alex sneered. 'Afraid not. My wife and daughter need to be in the equation.'

'Coming to that,' Bridge said. 'Soon as you put the money

down they'll be sent on to the walkway. You'll see them at the opposite side. Head back the way you came and they'll follow. Stay at your end with them until one of my men comes to pick the suitcase up and check it out. He'll put his thumb up and then you're free to go.'

Alex was quiet while he considered it. Superficially, it seemed to make sense. The obvious rationale, or the one he was meant to assume, was that once the exchange was made both parties would be separated by the motorway and could go their own ways unmolested. In his heart, he doubted Bridge would play it straight but figured he didn't have much choice other than to go along with it.

'OK.' Alex swallowed hard. That little word sounded so harmless but in saying it he risked everything dear to him.

'You really don't have much choice in the matter. So get started, and this time no games you can't win.'

Alex snapped back. 'Just remember I'll hunt you till I die if you hurt them.'

'Bring the money,' Bridge grunted and the phone went dead.

Alex sat a moment. The part that worried him was waiting for the thumbs up before they were supposed to move off the bridge. He glanced up at the walkway; it was so well-lit, they'd be really exposed up there. Giving himself a shake, he dialled Eddie's mobile. Eddie answered on the first ring and he told his friend how it was going down.

'I can only guarantee to watch your back properly once you're off the walkway,' Eddie warned. 'So get off there as soon as you can.'

'Don't worry, I will.'

Eddie wished him good luck and Alex ended the call. Focusing on the task at hand, he got out of the car, lifted the suit-case out of the boot. Gripping it tight, he made for the steps that ascended to the walkway.

At the top of the steps he paused. The long corridor stretched ahead for about a hundred yards. It was deserted and there was no movement at the far side. In the circumstances it looked to him like a tunnel to heaven or hell, the kind he'd read about in accounts of near-death experiences, that intermediary stage, the tunnel between this life and the next where you don't know quite what lies ahead. Way down beneath the bridge, in the real world, cars sped by. How he envied the passengers going about their normal lives while he stood here, his normal life held in suspension.

He began walking, eyes fixed on the far side. When he was ten yards in, he saw movement, realized it was Liz and Ann coming into view. Someone he didn't recognize was standing with them. He hoped Ann wouldn't react and run to him, start Bridge's men panicking. Encouraged that he could at least see them, he picked up his pace.

The walkway remained deserted. Half-way across, he halted, put the suitcase down. Following Bridge's instructions, he retraced his steps, the back of his neck prickling with anticipation. Several times he glanced over his shoulder, was relieved to see Liz and Ann were following. Ominously, another figure, dressed in a black anorak with the hood up, was walking twenty yards behind them.

Alex reached his end and turned around. Liz and Ann were only twenty-five yards away from him now, faces pale and drawn in the artificial light. They were moving at a snail's pace, holding on to each other like traumatized accident survivors unsure if what was happening was real. Their shadow stalker was bending over the suitcase checking the contents. When he was satisfied, he picked it up and started back his thumb in the air.

Relieved, Alex held out his arms, beckoned Liz and Ann to hurry to him, calling out they were safe now. Mother and daughter fell into his embrace and he could feel them trembling. His own emotions lurched between relief that they were safe and guilt because he was the one who had endangered them in the first place.

Liz broke away first. 'Why?' she asked, hurt and mystification in her voice. 'Why did they take us?'

Ann was looking up into his face, her eyes posing the same question as her mother. Alex swallowed hard; he wasn't looking forward to answering that question. But right now he wasn't sure the danger had passed, so he guided them to the steps.

As they descended the steps he muttered, 'There'll be time for explanations later. Right now it's best we get out of here.'

Crossing the car park, his eyes swept the area. Two people stepped out of the café, startling him. But they became harmless shadows in the night as they walked to their own car. He let out his breath. Not far to go now. Soon all this would dissolve into a bad nightmare.

He opened the passenger door. Ann started to climb into the back. Liz was only a step behind her. Nervous as an expectant father in a maternity ward, Alex fidgeted, wanting them to hurry.

His solicitude became an irrelevance when, out of the darkness behind him, a voice that was by now as familiar to him as it was chilling, made a mockery of any optimism he'd begun to feel.

'You went too far. You messed up my plans, not to mention taking my money.'

Ann froze, half-in, half-out of the car. Liz pulled her close. Alex's body tensed. Everything that had gone before in his life, all the possibilities that lay ahead, telescoped as he swung round.

Bridge was two yards away. The twisted grin on his face, more grotesque because of his swollen jaw, made his head more like a Halloween turnip than human. Alex's eyes riveted, not on his face, but on the gun he was holding by his side. Instinctively, he spread his arms like wings to protect Liz and Ann.

'Let them go, Bridge,' he pleaded. 'They're innocents. It was me who messed with you, not them.'

'Should have thought of that before.' Bridge stated, his voice bitter. 'But it's only you I'm interested in. But for you I'd have left the country yesterday. Ironic, isn't it? Just another day and you wouldn't have found me.'

The gangster paused. His voice changed again, from bitter to venomous. 'Right now, I'm wondering if I should kill or just maim you. What do you think? Got a preference?'

Bridge was playing with him, wanting to see him afraid. Alex wondered where Eddie was. He wanted to shout out but the gangster was too close, might panic and shoot. He needed to gain more time, so he gathered his courage, forced his voice deeper.

'Do what you have to do but be a man for once and let my daughter and her mother get clear. They don't want to see this.'

His lack of fear seemed to throw Bridge for a moment. Taking advantage, Alex turned to the females who were still holding on to each other.

'Liz, get Ann out of here now.'

Liz hesitated. She looked to be in shock and he could see tears forming in her eyes.

'Do it, you silly bitch,' he shouted, hating himself for it but knowing he'd have to shake her out of it, make her react.

Liz recoiled, her eyes bewildered, but his harsh words served their purpose because she started to walk away, pulling Ann with her. Both looked back at him, agonized, like two refugees being forced on to a road they had no wish to travel.

Bridge watched, a stupid grin on his face. The hand that held the gun started to rise.

'Time's run out for you, Alex, and you'll never really know whether your little darlings got away. I can still gun them down.'

'Not true!'

The words came out of the darkness behind the gangster. Alex recognized Eddie's voice. Bridge's gun hand froze. He was wondering whether it was worth taking a chance, finishing what he had started.

The gangster glanced over his shoulder. His earlier confidence deflated when Eddie loomed into view holding the shotgun. Slowly, in the interest of self-preservation, Bridge lowered his gun hand.

'Wise decision,' Eddie called out.

Alex almost laughed with relief. 'It never rains but it pours, eh Charlie? This just isn't your week.'

Bridge faced Alex. The temptation to take a chance was there in the body language. Tension hung on the night air. Over at the café, a door opened and a girl's high-pitched laugh seemed to come from another world to mock them.

Eddie spoke again. 'Get out of here while you've still got legs to carry you.'

Bridge, with one last menacing glance at Alex, turned around. He started to walk in a semicircle around Eddie, his gun held low. Eddie traced his movements with the shotgun. There was a savage, macabre primitivism in the way they watched each other.

'You're a lucky man, Doc,' Bridge hissed over his shoulder. 'But luck changes. I'll be back for you. Just think of me like one of those illnesses you can never cure.'

'You are an illness,' Alex called after him. 'You're as sick as they come.'

Liz and Anne had crept back and Eddie joined them. All four watched in silence as the gangster climbed the steps on to the bridge. At the top he turned and stared down at the car park.

'Don't worry,' Eddie said, for the females' sake. 'He can't see us.'

Alex hugged Liz and Anne. 'For a minute there I thought I was gone. Thanks pal.'

'Let's get out of here,' Eddie said as he watched Bridge progress along the walkway to the other side.

Liz, coming out of shock now that the danger had diminished, suddenly broke Alex's embrace and found her voice.

'What have you got us into, Alex?'

'It's a long story. No time for it now. I'll tell you later.'

'It better be good. By God, it had better be good.'

Anne was watching their faces, trying to read their lips in the poor light. Her eyes were wide with confusion. Alex pulled her closer to him, stroked her hair.

'We'll go back to my place,' Eddie said. 'It'll be safer there. He doesn't know who I am.'

'Thank God you came in time,' Alex said.

Eddie grunted. 'The shotgun wasn't loaded, by the way.'

'Didn't think so,' Alex said, grimacing. 'Knew you wouldn't risk a murder charge.'

'I'll drive back in my own car, Alex. You take Liz and Ann in yours. We'll use the back roads just in case they're waiting on the motorway.'

A minute later they were pulling out of the car park, Alex driving the lead car. He was grateful that Liz and Ann were so exhausted they fell asleep. If she was rested, Liz would be more receptive later, when he had to explain the trouble he'd brought her to her door.

CHAPTER 25

Eddie's apartment wasn't big enough for four but it was a safe haven in a troubled time. Ann was still dog-tired, kept clinging to her father, her ordeal clearly affecting her. Liz made her a cup of hot chocolate and put her to bed in the spare room. Alex followed them in to say goodnight. He had come so close to losing them and, as he leaned over to kiss his daughter, his tears were those of guilt as well as relief. Hiding the depth of his emotion, he followed Liz out of the bedroom. At the door, he paused to blow his daughter a kiss. She gave him a smile and signed goodnight and that she loved him. It made him feel worse.

Eddie and Liz were in the kitchen drinking coffee. Both looked white and exhausted. Eddie handed him a cup of coffee and he drank it gratefully, hoping the steam rising from the hot liquid would mask his tears. He sensed Liz was studying him, impatient for an explanation.

Eddie spoke first. 'You can stay here as long as you like. It's a bit cramped but I'll be out at work most of the time.'

Liz's eyes drifted from Alex to Eddie. 'That's nice of you. You're a good friend but I think I'll have to go home tomorrow. Ann has school and I have to go to work as well. We'll just have to put this behind us, return to normal. I'm sure routine will be the best thing for Ann after what's happened to her.'

Both men were silent. She saw the meaningful look pass

between them, surmised there was something they were reluctant to tell her, something she wasn't going to like.

His voice hoarse, Alex said quietly, 'You can't go home, Liz, because we don't know if they'll come for you again.'

Liz's eyes widened. 'You're saying we can never go home?'

Alex lowered his head, mumbled, 'It wouldn't be safe, not now.'

Liz's hand went to her mouth. She'd just been through one ordeal, thought it was over and done with, that she could return to normal. Now she was being told her whole life was upside down. She didn't cry but the tears weren't far away.

Eddie, sensing that she and Alex needed to be alone, took his cue and moved to the door.

'You need to talk this out,' he said, addressing both equally. 'I'll bed down on the sofa and see you in the morning.'

As soon as he was gone Liz sank into a chair, rested her elbows on the kitchen table, put her head in her hands as though she wished to shut the world out. Sheepishly, Alex lowered himself into a chair next to hers, stretched out a hand, touched her shoulder consolingly. Her head shot up, her eyes emotional firestorms as she looked into his.

'You need to tell me everything, Alex, right from the start and hope that I understand how you could have got us into such a mess.'

Alex reddened. Guilt swarmed over him like an army of grotesque insects intent on consuming any feeling of decency remaining in his body. He swallowed hard. The time had come to tell it all. No matter how bad it made him look, he owed her at least that.

'I made a foolish mistake,' he muttered, conscious of the throb in his throat. 'That led on to more mistakes. Bridge tested me, played me like a fish and in the end, when he had me, I could do nothing because he threatened to hurt you and Ann.' He hesitated. 'I need you to forgive me, Liz. I need it badly.'

'Then tell me from the beginning,' she said, face and voice impassive. 'I need to know it all. Be specific.'

He rubbed his tired eyes, met her unrelenting gaze. 'OK, everything. Right from the beginning.'

He told her it all, the photographic evidence they'd built against him, his attempt to pay them off, the final blow when they'd threatened those close to him. There were tears in his eyes but he felt a little better in the telling, as though confessing was cathartic for him, the way the land is fresh after a downpour.

'Right at the start, I was a fool,' he declared at the end, with a long sigh. 'Bridge built up the pressure but it all stemmed from my initial pride.'

Liz's brows knitted into a frown. She hadn't interrupted as he'd revealed the magnitude of his tribulations, his contrition. Now, he could see her weighing it in the scales of her judgement. All he could do was pray she'd understand and find it in her heart to forgive him. When she reached across the table, took his hand in hers and gave him hope, relief gushed through him like a torrent of pure water.

'Well, Alex, there's no doubting you were a fool to pay them off in the first place but you were definitely not a fool when it came to trying to protect us. I saw enough of Bridge's character to know, even if you'd told the police, that there was no guarantee he'd leave us alone. In fact, I'd say the opposite was more likely. The man's a psychopath. Even beyond the prison walls, he'd have influence over weak-minded followers.'

'Thank God you understand, at least,' Alex said. 'But can you forgive me?'

She gripped his hand more tightly, half-smiled, said softly: 'Your intentions were well-meaning, if misguided, so of course you're forgiven. Who's to say I wouldn't have reacted the same way in the circumstances?'

Alex sighed. 'But there's one thing nothing can help, and that's my responsibility for the injured prison officer. As I told you, that's why I went after Bridge's money. Stupidly, I wanted to try and make up for what I'd done. I never thought Bridge could possibly find out and come for you and Ann. More fool me.'

'The officer's injury is something you'll have to learn to live with. If you dwell on it you'll go crazy '

Alex cast his eyes down to the floor. 'Trouble is it's him who's living with it and I'll always know that. You think maybe I should just go to the police and confess everything?'

'What good would that do now? They'd have to sentence you no matter what the mitigating circumstances were. It could affect your daughter, set her back. What good would you be to her locked up?'

'But can I live with it?'

'We'll live with it,' Liz said, her jaw set. 'We'll have to go away, for now at least. It'll mean Ann changing schools, me changing jobs, but there's no other way if that man is likely to come after us again.'

'You'd do that,' Alex said, surprised.

Liz threw back her hair, looked him straight in the eye. 'Do we have any choice?'

He reached out, touched her cheek. 'I certainly want to be with you and Ann. Always have.'

'Then we'll do what I've suggested. Now go and make sure your daughter's OK. She's been through such a lot I'm worried about her.'

Alex stood, kissed Liz on the forehead and left the kitchen feeling more optimistic than he had done for a long time. There was a chance now that he could salvage something from the wreckage of his recent life. To help him do that, he'd have the two people he loved most in the world beside him.

Ann's bedside light was on, a habit he knew she'd long outgrown. Since it hadn't been on when he'd said goodnight, she must have switched it on herself. Yet she seemed to be sleeping peacefully enough. He decided to leave her to rest but, as he was about to retreat, her eyes opened and she smiled up at him. It was the same smile he remembered from years ago, when she was an infant and he'd crept into her bedroom and she'd pretended to be asleep only to open her eyes at the last minute. Remembering that game and so much more, emotion welled up inside him for what he'd put her through.

'You OK, darling?' he asked, leaning over so she could read his lips.

She must have read his emotion as well as his lips because she signed: 'Don't look so sad. I'm fine now.'

Since she seemed wide awake, he sat down on the bed. 'Try to get some sleep, Ann. You're quite safe now. Those men will never come near you and your mother again.'

'Why did they want to hurt you?' she signed, shifting her position so she was closer to him.

It wasn't a question he was prepared for. How did you tell your daughter, who thought you were just about perfect, that you were far from it? How did you explain evil?

'They're bad men, Ann. Most people are good and we don't often meet nasty people but sometimes, not very often at all really, our paths cross theirs. I was just unlucky and they thought they would hurt me by taking you and Mum.'

It was an improvised answer, perhaps not the best but it had been a direct question and he'd had to explain events somehow without going into the more unsavoury aspects, risking disturbing her. Fortunately, Anne seemed to accept it.

She signed. 'Don't worry, Dad, the one called Bridge won't be around to hurt us again.'

'Won't he?' he said gently, indulging her.

But Ann, wise enough to interpret his motive, shook her head sternly.

'Seriously, he won't. He's going away.'

Alex knew that was true because Bridge had said so and had held him responsible for delaying his departure. But was his daughter just romancing, using it as a form of denial to cope with the reality of the danger to which she'd been exposed?

'How do you know that, Ann?'

She grinned coyly, signed, 'He was on his mobile phone and he didn't know I was watching him through a window.'

'You read his lips! So what did he say?'

'He said he'd have to delay going to Portugal until next week. He mentioned a place. It was Vigo.'

'Did he now?' Alex mused, possibilities running through his head.

'It means we'll all be safe, doesn't it?' Ann signed, an anxious look on her face because of her father's faraway look.

Her concern jolted him out of it. He'd think about those possibilities later. For now, he concentrated on his daughter.

'Yes, Ann. There's no need to worry if he's going away.'

He didn't like lying to his daughter. As long as Bridge was alive, he knew their lives wouldn't be secure, no matter where they, or he, went. One little detail might give them away, bring Bridge's vengeance tumbling down on their heads. His daughter was happy with her life. They were going to have to disrupt it, take her away from her friends. He wanted to explain it carefully but he didn't have the heart.

'We're all going to live together,' he said, compromising. 'You'd like that wouldn't you? And we're going to go away for a while to celebrate.'

Her eyes lit up and he hated himself for his deceit. Before she had a chance to comment, in order to hide his embarrassment he embraced her and said goodnight.

The seed of an idea began to blossom as he made his way back to the kitchen. Liz noticed his distant look.

'Ann all right,' she asked anxiously.

'Fine!' He decided to come straight out with it because he'd hidden too much from her. 'Actually she's just given me an idea, a way of getting Bridge out of our lives for good.'

She glared at him, anger and disbelief intermingling. 'Come on! You're surely not going to get involved again? Not after all he's put us through.'

'No fear of me doing that, but if it works we may have to only make a temporary move, an extended holiday.'

'I'm all for anything that helps us to settle back here,' she said, calming down. 'But you'll have to tell me everything before I agree to anything that might cause us grief.'

He sat down at the table and she joined him. He began by explaining Hussein's visit to his house, the man's grief over what Bridge had done to his daughter, his burning thirst for revenge, finished with his belief that, if he passed on what Ann had just told him to Hussein, he would deal with Bridge in his own, no doubt violent way. The outcome would be that Bridge would be gone from their lives for good.

At first Liz was hesitant. 'You're sure we have to take things that far?'

'You've seen the man. This is the only way we can be sure we won't have to keep looking over our shoulders, that Ann's completely safe. We've already agreed if we told the police the likelihood is he'd get at us from jail. We've already seen how he can do that, haven't we?'

'I don't like the idea of operating outside the law,' she mused. 'But I'd go along with it as long as you're not involved, other than telling this Hussein character where you think Bridge is.'

'Then it's agreed,' Alex said. 'I'll see Hussein but meantime we'll make arrangements to move somewhere safe just as we'd planned.'

'Let's hope it's only temporary.' Liz said wistfully. 'I like living in this area.'

'Then Hussein's our man, our best chance.'

CHAPTER 26

Sitting at the head of the long table, Ali Hussein studied Alex, his dark eyes immobile and probing. His sons, who were also seated while Alex remained standing, regarded him with an intensity which equalled their father's. He didn't like what he was doing and right now he felt like a miscreant awaiting the judgement of a hastily mustered court trying to decide whether his story was truthful or not.

'Forgive me but this is not just a fantasy of your daughter's?' Hussein asked.

'I know my daughter,' Alex replied. 'Coincidentally, she has been to a place near Vigo on a family holiday, so she recognized the name when Bridge said it.'

Hussein momentarily broke eye contact, smoothed out a wrinkle in the white tablecloth.

'You know I will kill him,' he said.

'That is why I have come to you,' Alex answered. 'You have the resources I lack.'

'You want rid of him so your family can have peace?'

'Exactly. Even if he is imprisoned, he can strike out. You've heard my story. You can see why I am afraid for my family.'

Hussein placed his hands flat on the table. His eyes moved over each of his five sons in turn. None spoke but each gave a slight nod of his head.

The family had made their decision. Hussein sealed it when he stood up and extended his hand. Alex shook it.

'Consider him already dead,' Hussein declared with an air of finality, 'and yourself innocent in this matter. Nothing said today goes beyond these four walls. I speak for my sons as well.'

'Good luck,' Alex mumbled, then turned away and made his way out of the restaurant.

The idea of plotting a death, even of a man like Bridge, in such a cool, calculated fashion, felt bizarre. It seemed a far cry from the high-minded Hippocratic oath he'd taken when he became a doctor. It gave him no pleasure, even though it had become necessary.

Driving away from the restaurant, he continued to have mixed feelings. Hussein's words about his innocence reverberated in his head, partly because he wanted to believe it was true, partly because, in spite of them, he felt sullied. As he pulled into the car park outside Middlesbrough police station, he hadn't come to terms with it. Was he really doing the right thing or was this another case of flawed judgement on his part? His track record wasn't too good in that department, was it?

He concentrated on maintaining a show of outward composure when a young policeman in uniform showed him into DI Johnson's office. If past experience with the detective was anything to go by, he would have to stay sharp-witted when he faced the caustic, accusatory comments the policeman was sure to conjure from whatever he said.

'Come to confess?' Johnson's opening gambit, as Alex sat down in the chair he was offered, was the kind he'd expected.

'Just keeping you informed of my intended movements,' Alex stated, 'as requested.'

Johnson's blue eyes mocked him. 'Running but not hiding kind of thing. That it?'

Alex ignored the sarcasm. 'I'm back with my wife and

daughter and we want to take a long holiday, probably some-where near the sea. We may even make it a permanent move.'

'Sea air to clean out the lungs and whatever else may be clogged up. Does it really work, Doctor Macdonald?'

'Just letting you know,' Alex said, rising from the chair.

Johnson stood up, squared his wide shoulders. 'Ring me when you know precisely when and where.'

'Sure,' Alex said, unenthusiastically. He headed for the door, disconcerted by those accusatory blue eyes which followed him and seemed capable of penetrating the false edifices he'd built.

'Suspended from your job, aren't you?' Johnson called out as his hand clasped the door handle.

Alex turned. Couldn't the man just let it go, resist a last dig at him? His own guilt was heavy enough without this persistent niggling.

'Mistakes at work suggest a man with a lot on his mind,' the detective continued. Then, surprisingly, his voice softened. 'Bridge got to you, didn't he? What was it? Did he threaten your family? Is he still threatening? Is that why you're upping sticks?'

'You should write a novel, Detective,' Alex answered. 'You've got the imagination for it.'

Johnson sighed. 'Well, at least I've done my research. I've read your army record. You were a good soldier, no black marks. In fact it's quite a distinguished record. My so-called imagina-tion tells me you wouldn't help Bridge willingly, that he got to you. Why not come clean, Alex? We can help you if you were put under pressure. Or if you are still being put under pressure.'

Alex grimaced, opened the door. As he walked out he called over his shoulder, 'Write that book, Detective. It could be a best-seller.'

Driving out of the car park, he was far from feeling as cocky and confident as those last words to the policeman had made him sound. In the army he'd been self-disciplined, respected rules because he understood that, if you didn't, chaos ensued. It was a small step for the intellect to extend that concept to society itself. Now, having stepped outside those boundaries, he had to hope that Hussein would do a good job and keep him and his family out of it as he'd promised. His life had been in enough chaos recently to do for a lifetime.

CHAPTER 27

The sun was at its highest. In the plaza of the small village three miles from Vigo the shopkeepers were rolling down the blinds in preparation for the afternoon siesta. A shadow of the church lay across the cobbled stones. Encompassed by the shade it afforded, a group of old men sat in silence on the church steps, as though waiting for something to happen to break the routine pattern of their days.

Bella sat at a table outside one of the two cafés that faced on to the square. With a lazy, circular action, she rubbed suntan lotion into her bare shoulders. When she'd finished she adjusted the straps on her dress and put her sunglasses back on. Across the table her brother laid down his English newspaper and stretched. He was wearing a yellow T-shirt and white slacks. His face and the exposed parts of his flesh were tanned to the same shade as his sister's skin. Both looked vibrantly healthy.

Bella raised her glass. 'What could be better than this, brother?'

Bridge slouched in his chair, crossed his legs, swatted a fly hovering on the rim of his glass which sparkled in the sun. He gestured expansively.

'Who could have imagined this when we were kids with nothing in the world except each other?'

Bella regarded him closely. 'You're happy, then?'

He sighed, considered her question. 'Sometimes I miss the old dodging and weaving but then I think back to the prison, boxed up with all those lowlifes, my skin the colour of chalk.' He examined a tanned forearm, stared up at the cloudless blue sky. 'Thank God I have a clever sister who got me out. This last month has been so good.'

Bella smiled. 'It certainly wasn't easy for me living out at that stinking farmhouse miles from anywhere, lying to the doctor to cover my movements while I was finding his weaknesses and putting the plan together. Gloria was my alias but *gloria in excelsis* it certainly wasn't.'

'Yes, the good doctor,' Bridge mused, a hard glint in his eye. 'I haven't forgotten him. In the end he nearly blew it for me. I have that in mind, of course.'

'You're not going to let it go?' she said, looking concerned.

Bridge laughed. 'Wouldn't be me if I did, would it? I have my pride and I promised the bastard. For now though, I'll let him stew.'

'Up to you,' Bella said. 'Just don't do anything that gives us away. I like the life we're leading.'

'Trust me,' Bridge told her.

People started to leave the adjoining tables and the waiters were hovering in the background ready to close up and enjoy their own siesta. Bridge drained his glass.

'You ready?' Bella asked.

'Think I'll walk back,' he said and patted his stomach. 'It ain't far and it's time I had some exercise. You take the car.'

Bella stood, pushed back a loose strand of red hair. 'We'll have lunch by the pool. I'll have it ready by the time you get back. Maybe we can drive into Vigo later, meet some people, make new friends.'

Bridge followed her out of the café. He watched her walk down the narrow alley which led to the street where they'd parked, then took another direction himself. Walking as briskly as the heat would allow, he emerged from the village on to the winding country road that crept up into the hills. Their villa was about a mile away, enough exertion in this heat.

Though he was blowing hard, he considered he'd never felt better in his life. Anonymity had its advantages, even for someone with as big an ego as his. He'd lied to his sister, of course. True, he liked it here, could settle for a while but you couldn't deny your own nature. Bella probably knew that eventually he'd have to get back to his old ways. You couldn't sit still in life. Onwards and upwards was the way to go. There was always more money to be made. Deep down Bella knew. All that talk back at the café was a bit of a fantasy.

The road he was walking led nowhere, came to a dead halt. There were three villas like their own on the way up the hill but theirs was the highest, near the dead end. After he'd gone about a quarter-mile, Bella passed him in the car and waved. He lengthened his stride, pushing against the steep incline.

Half-way up he rested. Looking west, beyond an expanse of countryside, was the sea. He was able to work out roughly which way England lay. The mother country seemed far away, his past more remote by the day, even in the short time they'd been here. Maybe it was the heat getting to him, or the awareness of distances from his vantage point, but standing here made him aware of his own mortality, that nothing he'd done in his past was of any consequence, except that it had made him a pile of money. He laughed at himself. Apart from his sister, wasn't money and the adrenalin rush he achieved making it, all that mattered?

The hum of a car engine interrupted his reverie. He watched a sleek, black car creeping up the incline behind him. Apart from their own, it was the first car he'd seen on this road and he figured it must belong to one of the villas. Perhaps a neighbour was returning home for a quick siesta. As it swept past him, he noticed two men were sitting in the front. The one in the passenger seat waved to him, a gesture he returned. Then the vehicle disappeared around a curve and he forgot about it, concentrated on maintaining his stride, his muscles starting to protest against the unaccustomed workload.

When he came to the last villa he noticed the same car parked on the road. The window blinds were down and he figured his theory about the car's occupants taking a siesta was right.

The last bend in the road was visible now. Soon he would be able to see his destination. Encouraged, he pushed on, shirt damp with sweat, hoping that that was a sign the weight was coming off. The villa came into view, the length of a football field away. Bella was standing beside the pool in her bikini. She waved at him and disappeared inside.

Stomach rumbling in anticipation of the food she would have ready for him, he renewed his efforts but slowed when he heard a noise behind him. In spite of the heat, he felt himself go cold. Senses tuning in, he turned. The car that he'd seen earlier was charging up the incline, its engine roaring like a living thing stirred to anger. He froze. His mind cried out danger but there was nowhere to run or hide and the beast was almost on top of him. With a squeal of brakes, it stopped alongside him. A cloud of dust encircled him and pricked at his eyes.

The doors opened and two men got out. The nearest one, slim, sleek and dark, was holding a jacket over his arm. He lifted it slightly showing the barrel of his gun. Time expanded as Bridge fixed on the weapon. His bowels churned and he wondered if this was it, if his uncustomary thoughts on mortality only minutes ago had been a premonition.

The other man, the driver, squat, muscle-bound, dark-skinned like his partner, came round the car and opened the back door.

'Get in,' the sleek one ordered.

For a brief moment, Bridge was relieved that he was still alive. He thought about running but the terrain and their aura of capability dissuaded him. He climbed into the car, tried to calm himself with the knowledge that at least they hadn't killed him instantly, which suggested they wanted something from him and maybe were open to negotiation.

'What is it you want?' he asked as the one with the gun climbed in the back seat beside him and stuck the weapon in his side.

Neither man answered and the silence was chilling. Something about these two, not least the expensive suits, told him they weren't just run-of-the-mill kidnappers.

He tried again. 'Who sent you?'

Again no answer. Then the squat one started the engine and drove towards the villa.

'The woman's already in the house,' he said to his partner.

'She won't suspect anything. We just walk in,' the sleek one responded.

Bridge, growing increasingly afraid because it was as if he didn't exist to these men, as if he were already dead, muttered, 'Whoever's paying you, I'll pay more. I've got plenty.'

Still neither man answered. Bridge couldn't understand their impassivity. Could this be personal with them? Most people he had dealings with responded when you mentioned money but these two hadn't even shown a flicker of emotion. Maybe then it was something personal involved here. But what the hell could they want? Why hadn't they just shot him?

The car pulled on to the concrete drive at the front of the building, halted beside Bridge's vehicle. Sleek jabbed the gun into his ribs.

'Out! Now!'

Bridge did as he was told. Sleek stood beside him, his jacket draped casually over his arm covering his gun. Squat, mean-while, opened the boot, reached in, lifted out a small brown-paper bag. His actions puzzled Bridge. What was going on here?

The door was wide open. Sleek pushed Bridge ahead and all three entered the villa.

'Call your sister,' Squat ordered as they stood in the hallway.

He thought about disobeying but one look at the men's adamantine features disposed of that idea. Besides, Bella, with her superior intellect, might be able to talk to these two Neanderthals better than he could. Perhaps this was to all to do with her anyway, since they obviously knew she was his sister.

'Bella!' he shouted. 'Come here, Bella.'

Nothing happened. The smell of cooking drifted from the kitchen. Sleek's nose twitched as he caught the aroma.

Sleek nodded at Squat. 'Look around,' he said. 'I'll take this one into the living-room.'

Squat reached inside his jacket. Bridge caught a glimpse of his shoulder holster. A Beretta appeared in his hand as he started down the hall. Meanwhile, Sleek pushed Bridge into the living-room, made him sit and sat down opposite. He looked cool, as though he was right at home, the air of a professional about him, someone who'd done this many times. Earlier, when he'd been offered money, there'd been no reaction. Bridge didn't know what to think or do. He'd heard that real pros, the contract killers, couldn't be bought off, honoured the original agreement because they valued their reputation in the market place. He'd heard of such men but never met them.

Minutes dragged by, the clock on the marble mantelpiece marking each one audibly, as though to remind Bridge he might not have many more left. He wanted to say something but he sensed Sleek wouldn't have any of it. At last, Squat entered the room looking perplexed.

'Searched everywhere,' he said, rubbing his neck. 'Can't find the bitch.'

Sleek thought for a moment, then said, 'We saw her come up in the car. She must be around.'

'Nowhere to be seen,' Squat said. 'Maybe she saw us coming, got suspicious and found a hidey-hole.'

Sleek looked at Bridge. He put the gun down, reached inside his jacket pocket, drew out a pair of handcuffs and threw them at his partner.

'Put them on him,' he said. 'We'll figure her out later.'

Squat did as he was told. Bridge complied without fuss because Sleek had the gun pointed at him and he sensed it wouldn't make any difference what he did or said since these two were set on a course of action and nothing was going to divert them. A straitjacket of fear enveloped him because he was at their mercy, more so with the cuffs on. His only hope was that they had purposes other than killing on their minds.

When Squat finished putting the cuffs on he stepped away. Then Sleek stood up, strolled lethargically across the room, the gun at his side. He looked down at Bridge from under his lazy, lizard lids with an air of total boredom, as though mundane routine had sapped his energy and enthusiasm.

'Cover the door in case the bitch is around,' he told Squat.

Bridge watched Squat do as he was told and take up a covering position. Everything felt so wrong; he wished he'd made a move before they'd put those cuffs on him. The strait-jacket of fear tightened, constricted his throat. He found his voice but it was the croak of a man with a desert thirst pleading to the unrelenting skies for sustenance.

'I'm a rich man. If it's a ransom you want—'

'Open your mouth!' Sleek ordered.

Bridge shook his head, tried to rise. Sleek put his open palm on his face and pushed him back down.

'Do it!'

Bridge complied, gaze fixed on the gun which was hanging loose at Sleek's side. His stomach churned and his bowels started to loosen but his mind clung to the hope that all this was just to frighten him, not to kill him.

'Close your eyes!'

Instead, Bridge shut his mouth, blinked and blustered, 'You don't know who you're dealing with here.'

Sleek smiled, showed a set of yellow teeth which were incongruous with the rest of his appearance. 'I'm told I'm dealing with someone who thinks deaf means dumb. Who's the dumb one, Bridge?'

It took a moment, but he remembered that the doc's daughter was deaf and knew in the same instant how they'd found him. His heart sank to fresh depths. One error, one small neglect where the girl was concerned, was all it had been. Bella had warned him. Why hadn't he finished the girl off then and there?

'Please don't kill me,' he mumbled, knowing now death was the most likely outcome. 'I can top whoever's paying you. The doctor can't be paying much.'

Even to his own ears he sounded pathetic, a man stripped of his dignity. Sleek, with that same of boredom, brought the gun up, pushed the barrel against Bridge's lips.

'Mouth open again! Eyes closed!'

Bridge shook his head. Sleek, moving swiftly and with economy, swiped him hard across the face with the gun barrel.

'Do it!' he commanded, animated for the first time.

Whimpering with pain, Bridge obeyed. Bizarrely, a childhood memory, sitting in a dentist's chair and kicking out, floated into his mind through the pain and panic. But this was no dentist's chair and Sleek had the air of an executioner.

'Don't move, just listen,' Sleek hissed. He paused dramatically for a moment, then continued: 'Remember a girl called Hussein, do you?'

For Bridge it was the moment of total comprehension. He had the missing pieces that created the chain of events that had put him in this mess; the doc had gone to Hussein or vice versa and they'd planned this together. With that understanding, he knew he had not the smallest chance because Hussein was a rich man and would be paying well.

Before he could react to the question he felt something in his mouth, something soft and powdery that penetrated his throat and windpipe. He started to choke and was compelled to swallow. His eyes were wide open as he gasped for air. Sleek gripped his hair, pulled his head back, forced more of the powdery substance into his mouth and he thought he was going to black out. Coughing and spluttering, he fought his way back from the brink, became aware that Sleek and Squat were hovering over him like visitors at a deathbed waiting for the moment.

'It's pure heroin, courtesy Ali Hussein. He wanted you to know that,' Squat said. 'It'll drag out a bit but you'll be as good as dead before we're gone.'

'Nothing personal on our part,' Sleek added, then sideswiped him with the gun barrel.

Bridge felt himself tumbling into a black hole. Somewhere in the darkness there was a pinprick of light. He desperately wanted to get to it but it was receding too rapidly.

'That's only half the job done, so half the money,' Squat complained. 'Let's find the bitch.'

Sleek shook his head. 'Another day. We've spent too much time here. Got to dump the car yet.'

'Bitch got lucky,' Squat grumbled and followed Sleek outside.

'Maybe,' Sleek said. 'But it could be she's resourceful and we've underestimated her because she's a woman.'

CHAPTER 28

Bella had seen her brother coming up the incline just as she stepped out of the pool. She had waved, then gone inside and up to the bedroom to put on her bathrobe. That was when her first piece of luck kicked in: from the upstairs window she noticed the car coming too fast up the hill. Her second piece of luck was that the binoculars were conveniently placed on the window ledge, no more than an arm's length away. She focused on the car as it drew up alongside her brother.

Alongside the luck, instinct played its part now, because something in the casual confidence of the men who got out of the car set off warning bells. Her brother's posture was wrong too, the way he shrank away from the taller man. What was he afraid of? She swivelled the binoculars on to the man. That was when the third piece of luck blessed her with just the briefest glimpse of the gun Sleek was concealing under the jacket over his arm. As her brother climbed into the car, she fought against a tide of panic. Think, she told herself as the car headed up to the house. There's always a way.

One weapon. They kept one loaded weapon, a pump-action shotgun hidden at the bottom of the old well in the garden, nothing nearer at hand because they'd felt safe here. Get it, Bella's instincts screamed. Already she could hear the car pulling on to the drive.

She bounded down the stairs and was running through the

back door when she heard them come through the front. She closed the door behind her, then ran across the flower-beds to the old well. In one fluid movement she grasped the rope and went over the side. Holding on tight, she used her feet to gain purchase against the side wall and lowered herself into the depths.

The well was deep but dry this time of year. She felt her feet hit the bottom and let go of the rope. It was dark, too dark. The light from above wasn't nearly good enough. She remembered that Charles had used a torch when he'd clambered down. Hoping her eyes would adjust, she waited as vital seconds ticked by. There was only a little improvement in her vision so she began to feel her way around.

Charles had told her the shotgun was in a cavity behind a stone that protruded more than the others. She got down on her knees, used her hands to feel for the stone, froze when she heard a noise above her. She glanced up. The silhouette of a man's figured blotted out the patch of blue sky at the mouth of the well. She scrambled to the side, flattened herself against the wall as the figure stared down into the depths.

He soon disappeared and she let her breath go, resumed her frantic searching. At last her fingers discovered a stone slab protruding more than the others. She manoeuvred it until it slid away, then hauled out the waterproof bag in which her brother had placed the weapon. She removed the shotgun, used her bathrobe belt to bind it tight to her body and felt for the rope. Luckily, the surface of the walls wasn't flat so there were enough footholds to help her ascend. But she still had to feel for them with her feet. Progress was slow, agonizingly so because she was terrified for her brother up there in the house.

At the top, she peered over the side to check that nobody was in the garden, then pulled herself out. She ran straight for the house, went in through the back door, flattened herself against the kitchen wall.

A bird in the garden chirruped contentedly but she couldn't hear any other sound as she crept down the hallway. When she was halfway to the front room the car's engine purred into life. Relief that the men must be leaving vied with a fearful apprehension. What might they have done to her brother? In case one of the men had stayed in the house, perhaps hoping to trap her, she continued cautiously, dreading what she might find.

That dread was justified when she found her brother on the living-room floor, back propped against the sofa. His eyes were open and she dared to hope, figuring they'd beaten him but had at least left him alive. As she rushed across the room and saw his eyes, a worm of doubt wriggled in her stomach. His eyes weren't right. They had that glazed look she'd seen in the eyes of drug addicts and they were black, as if an evil spirit had driven out the personality, left a void. Kneeling beside him, she cradled him in her arms. That was when she noticed the white powder on his lips and down his shirt front and knew what was wrong.

In spite of his condition her brother seemed to recognize her. He tried to speak and she had to lean closer.

'Hussein – Huss … ein.'

She understood then who had sent those men.

'How, my darling? How could he know?'

Her brother tried to answer but it was too much for him as the drug tightened its grip. Frustrated, with an effort he raised an arm and pointed to his ear. It was all he could manage before his eyes closed.

She was wasting time. She'd have to get him to a hospital and the quickest way would be to drive him herself. Tears streaming down her cheeks, she tried to haul him on to his feet, but he was too heavy and she collapsed on the floor. The phone was an arm's length from where she lay. She reached for it, called the emergency services, asked for an ambulance. Then, as she had done when they were kids without a grown-up to do it, on those occasions when she'd had to be both mother and father to him, she cradled him in her arms and stroked his hair. All the while a cauldron of bitterness boiled up inside her against those responsible for hurting her precious brother.

He died in her arms two minutes later. All Bella wanted to do was stay beside him, for ever. But she was too much of a fighter, an instinct for survival was too ingrained. Hit the world back harder than it hits you had been her long-standing creed, as it had been her brother's.

She forced herself to stand. Tearfully, she looked down on her brother for the last time and resolved that Hussein would pay, even if it cost her life. She walked out of the room, went upstairs, collected all she needed in a suitcase, lugged it down, bundled it into the car and drove away.

As the villa receded into the distance, she felt once again the pain of that little, lonely orphan girl abandoned by her mother. With Charles by her side, she'd made it through. Together they'd taken on the world, made something of themselves against the odds. Now, without him, without anyone of her own blood, the future seemed a lonely wasteland where she would have to venture alone. The ambulance passed her on the hill, its siren scream mocking any pretension that, for her, happiness could last. She didn't turn around, kept her eyes on the road, vowing vengeance as the tears streamed down her cheeks.

CHAPTER 29

It was a cold day in Scarborough, the wind blowing rain off the sea. Not many people were venturing on to the streets of the east coast resort today. Alex, braving the elements, called into a corner shop to buy some groceries and a newspaper. He stuffed the paper inside the plastic bag with the groceries, pulled his coat collar up and hurried back to the flats where he, Liz, and Ann had sequestered themselves while they waited to hear if the danger Bridge posed had dissolved and they could return to a normal life.

As he climbed the stairs to the top floor flat he couldn't help feeling this furtive existence was wrong. Was it his guilt resurfacing? He still had doubts about letting Liz persuade him to put his trouble behind him, ignore his conscience. For sure, he had no qualms about setting the dogs on Charles Bridge; the man deserved all he got in Alex's book. Deep down, what was bothering him was that he hadn't gone to the police right at the start. They would surely have helped him, and Officer Clark wouldn't have ended up injured. Instead of that, his main priority had been preserving his dignity and pride in the eyes of other people; it had been the weakness they'd used to rope him in. Could he live normally with that knowledge niggling at him for the rest of his days? That was the big question.

He let himself into the flat and walked through to the kitchen. His wife and daughter were seated close together at the kitchen table. It gave him a warm feeling to see them like that, to know he belonged to them, was a proper part of their lives again. Surely that bond, the warmth of his family, would drive out those feelings that had troubled him over the fortnight they'd been here? Well, he'd just have to try to reconcile himself to the past, learn to live with it, wouldn't he? If he didn't he'd be no good to anyone.

'We need a holiday in the sun,' he remarked as he hung his raincoat on the hook behind the door.

Liz smiled and handed him a towel to dry his hair. He gave her the bag and she emptied the contents on to the table.

'Don't worry. We're fine here.'

Ann signed. 'It's better than being at school.'

'Don't get too used to it, young lady,' Alex said, relaxing into a chair and supping the hot coffee Liz put in front of him. 'We'll be going back soon, I hope.'

Glad to be inside and out of the rotten weather, he picked the newspaper off the table and unfolded it. The main headlines were about the situation in Iraq, the front page apportioning guilt for the death of civilians, political leaders trying to wriggle away from facts. Spin seemed to be the new word for downright lies. It depressed him to see the prevarications, the avoidance of truth. Then it dawned on him he was hardly a man of integrity in a position to criticize, to pontificate about truth, having played hard and fast with the truth himself. Uncomfortable with that thought, he turned to the second page. A headline there screamed off the page and he quickly scanned the column.

When he'd finished reading, he put the paper down. Liz noticed his faraway look, sensed a change in him.

'What's wrong?' she said resting a hand on his shoulder.

He looked up, pointed at the headline. 'It's finished,' he said, voice neither elated nor sad, just flat.

She grabbed the paper, read the piece for herself. Alex

watched her growing relief as she comprehended what it meant for their future. She put the paper back on the table and sighed.

'So Bridge is dead from a massive overdose of heroin. Thank God we're free of him is all I can say.'

Alex grunted. 'He died the same way as Hussein's daughter, except his wouldn't have been a voluntary act. Grim, but a kind of justice.'

'Cheer up, Alex,' Liz said, noticing he was sombre. 'You look right down when you should be relieved. This was the only way we could guarantee our long-term safety, remember. We're free to live normal lives now.'

Alex wished he could be as buoyant as she was. Normal lives sounded good. Could it be that way for him?

'But will I ever be free of guilt, Liz? It's still there, you know. I'm not always aware of it, but it's like my shadow, always ready to put in an appearance whenever I think the sun's shining again.'

Tears, like small white pearls, formed in the corners of Liz's eyes.

'We've been over this. You're with me and your daughter. That should be enough. Time is a great healer. It'll all go away. We'll make it go away.'

He sighed. 'You were my healer in Iraq, Liz, but this time I'm not so sure you can work your magic.' Seeing how upset he'd made her, he cast his eyes down. 'But I know I've got to try to settle my mind. I know that.'

She wiped the tears away, then touched her daughter's shoulder to attract her attention and direct Alex's mind elsewhere.

'We'll be going home soon, Ann,' she said. 'Everything's going to be OK.'

Ann's face lit up. She looked across to her father and signed. 'Are you definitely going to live with us back home? Are you going to be a doctor again?'

Alex smiled. His troubles faded away when he looked at his daughter. Maybe Liz was right. Maybe he'd be all right.

'Yes, I'm going to live with you. I'll try to be a doctor again. Maybe I won't succeed but I'll try. If not, I'll find something. Don't you worry about it.'

'We'll all be happy,' Ann said, beaming at him.

She looked so innocent right at that moment, he wished time could stand still, that the world outside would never encroach, that his daughter would always be as happy. Nearly losing her and Liz had made him realize where he truly belonged. His time with Gloria seemed a bad dream now. He wondered how he could ever have imagined a future with her. Loneliness out there in his country house must have driven him mad. Thank God, she'd walked out. It would never have worked between them; he could see that now. In the middle of his reverie the phone rang in the bedroom. He looked at Liz.

'That'll be Eddie reporting in,' he told her as he rose and walked to the door. 'Apart from the landlady, he's the only one who knows where we're living.'

'You've probably heard?' Eddie's familiar voice said when Alex picked up in the bedroom.

'Yes, the matter's apparently been dealt with!'

'Our friend rang to confirm it. But they don't know where the other one, the female, is. Our man said to stay where you are another week or two to be on the safe side.'

'But there wasn't any threat from that direction, not to me.'

'Best to be on the safe side. The so-called professionals apparently slipped up but won't do that twice. They reckon they'll need another two weeks maximum.'

Alex was disappointed. He'd thought it was all behind him and they could go home. Still, like Eddie said, best to be safe.

'Suppose another two weeks won't hurt. Thanks, pal, for all the trouble you've gone to.'

'Chin up, old son,' Eddie answered. 'It'll soon be over.'

He returned to the kitchen with the news. Liz took it well and, when they told Ann they weren't going back yet, the prospect of more time off school didn't faze her unduly.

Later, when they were alone, Liz broached the subject again. 'What kind of woman would pursue it further? It was her brother, not she, who wasn't going to leave us to lead our lives in peace.'

'You saw her,' Alex said. 'How did she strike you?'

'She kept in the background. I only had brief glimpses. Not enough to know much about her.'

'It's enough to know that she was with her brother all the way,' Alex stated bitterly. 'I don't really think she'll be a threat but why take a chance on going back?'

'Two weeks maximum?'

'What Eddie was told.'

'Let's make the best of it, then.'

Alex forced a grin. Sometimes Liz's optimism was infectious. Perhaps it would be enough to chase away his demons.

CHAPTER 30

She could go anywhere. Money wouldn't be a problem. She was attractive, could maybe find a man she wanted to be with. They could travel the world, live hedonistic lives, reach old age together, ease their way to that final sunset. But she knew that that was the dream for another day. Reality was that wherever she went, whatever she did, her brother would always be there calling out to her and she would always want to answer his unspoken plea to avenge him. Their parents had abandoned them but she wouldn't abandon her brother, not even in death, because blood-ties counted. You took care of your own or you weren't human. Her parents had been inhuman but she wouldn't be. She'd complete the last task her brother would desire from her, then, maybe, if she survived, pursue those other dreams.

'More coffee, miss?' The air stewardess's cheerful voice interrupted her musing.

Bella held out her cup. When it was full she put it on the tray, studied the people on the plane. Most of them, she knew from their accents, were County Durham folk returning to the north from the big smoke.

When she'd left Spain a week before she'd used a false passport to fly to London. From the capital she could have gone anywhere in the world, lain low for a while, but she was impatient to do what she had to. She was pleased to be heading home, the way a wounded animal, hurt and alone, seeks the familiar.

As she glanced across the aisle she noticed two teenagers, a boy and girl. They were making wild hand-gestures and she thought it must be some stupid game they were playing to pass the time. They looked too old for that kind of frivolity to her. At their age she'd have been far too mature. She'd had to grow up quickly and put aside childish things. Dismissing them from her thoughts, she returned to her current concerns.

The pilot announced they were about to land, instructed the passengers to put on their seatbelts. The plane commenced its descent and Bella looked out of the window. Below, she could see runway lights, beyond them the lights of the Teesside conurbation. Those lights seemed to her pinpricks of optimism in the vast, mysterious darkness of a universe where chaos reigned and anything could happen. Where was Charles now in that inscrutable infinity?

The plane landed smoothly but disembarking procedures were tedious, more so in the light of tightened security owing to recent terrorist activities, but her passport was good and she had no trouble going through customs. She carried her one suitcase out of the building and climbed in the first taxi she saw.

'Where to?' the driver asked.

'The Bluebell Hotel in Middlesbrough. Acklam to be more precise. And don't take the long route because I know the area and the town too well to be deceived.'

She saw the man's eyebrows rise as he studied her in the mirror, knew he was thinking he'd picked up a right one this trip. She held his gaze and he didn't come back at her.

Before he was even into second gear he blasted on his horn and braked hard. Bella shot forward and had to reach out to check her momentum. She heard the driver cursing, the target of his abuse the two teenagers who'd been sitting across the aisle on the plane. They were strolling blithely along in front of the taxi like nature-lovers on a country stroll, unaware he had almost hit them.

'You OK, love?' the driver enquired. 'Those two must be deaf, daft or blind. Stepped right in front of me, they did. My own bleeding ticker went twice round the clock.'

'I'm OK,' she said and settled back into the seat. Good start, she told herself. Welcome home.

Somewhere on the road to the town she had a moment of revelation, a gift from the gods. The driver had been partly correct when he was sarcastic about the two teenagers. He'd got two out of three; they weren't daft or blind; they were deaf. All that hand gesticulating on the plane had been sign language, not a stupid game. She should have seen that, then she might have recalled before this that Alex Macdonald's daughter was deaf, that she was able to sign, also read lips. Poor Charles, in his last effort to communicate with her, had pointed to his ear. She figured he must have been trying to convey, as best he could, how they'd managed to find him.

The fatal day in the garden played back in her memory like a punishment. Charles had taken a call on his mobile. He'd turned to her and said everything was taken care of, that in a few days they'd be away to Vigo in Portugal. He said nobody else, not even those who'd been closest to him, knew their destination, because he'd fixed the flights and kept every detail to himself. They'd hire a villa in a quiet place. It would be as if they'd vanished off the face of the earth.

At the time they'd been facing the house. She'd suddenly looked up to see the Macdonald brat watching them from the bedroom where she and her mother were confined. The girl had drawn back and she could remember a brief presentiment, dismissed in the same instant because she didn't think the brat could possibly have known what they were discussing. She'd mentioned it to Charles though, but he hadn't worried. It was a bitter irony, one that sickened her, that she, who had looked out for her brother all her life, had neglected to get rid of the brat. Charles would still be alive if she had. Blaming herself, she brooded on her negligence for the rest of the journey.

When she'd paid the taxi driver she checked in to the Bluebell Hotel, bought a bottle of wine from the bar, went straight up to her room, undressed and got into bed. She settled back on the pillows and drank the wine. She had so much to think about. Macdonald had obviously co-opted Hussein to do his dirty work for him, thinking that would get him and his family off the hook. He must be gloating now but the fool had better think again. Nobody could hurt her brother and get away with it. Not while she was still breathing.

She'd had one target in mind when the plane landed but now she had two. Both Hussein and the doctor would have to be eliminated. Which one would she deal with first? The question revolved in her mind until the long journey and the effects of the wine eventually caught up with her she fell into a deep sleep.

CHAPTER 31

In the deserted cemetery a light wind flirted with the floral tributes for the dead. The same wind, like a playful ghost, lifted Hussein's coat tail as he strode down the pathway between the gravestones. He kept his head down, never once glanced towards the church where Bella waited in the shadows.

Ironies flooded into Bella's mind. Here she was, an atheist, sheltering in the shadows of the church while she waited to kill a man of another country's faith, who was here to visit a Christian grave. It reinforced her own sense of the world as a crazy, mixed-up place where rules were for the weak.

In the furthest corner of the cemetery Hussein kneeled down in front of a tall gravestone. Bella permitted herself a small smile, congratulating herself on her powers of recall. Everything was happening just as she remembered Hussein's daughter describing it to her when she'd cultivated the naïve young runaway for her brother. Hussein didn't have a clue that anyone knew about his lone, secret visits to this place every Thursday afternoon of his life. By chance his daughter had seen him enter the churchyard and discovered his secret but, fearing his wrath, had not told him she knew. Your sins will find you out. Only if, like Hussein, you care about them enough to hide them, was Bella's thinking.

After making sure they were alone Bella stepped out of the shadows. Without respect for the dead she walked over the graves, heading in a straight line for Hussein, who was facing away from her and oblivious to her presence even when she stood a yard behind him.

'It's a dirty, sordid, little secret you have there,' she said, conscious of the triumph ringing in her voice.

Surprised at the vitriolic intrusion in a place he would never have expected it, Hussein stumbled to his feet and turned. He stared at her, mystified. She knew he was wondering who this mad woman was. What was she talking about? Surely she must have mistaken him for someone else. Caught off balance, he looked like a little boy lost and she relished his discomfiture. It was the least he deserved and she played on it.

'Your sins will find you out. That's what the Christians say. This is a good place for your sins to find you out, isn't it?'

Still he didn't say anything, just stared. She could see enough concern in his face to know he understood what, in his case, her words implied. At the same time he wasn't sure it was any more than the ramblings of a crazy woman who'd coincidentally hit a home truth.

'Your daughter knew what a creep and hypocrite you were,' she stated, drawing him in piece by piece.

As though struck by an invisible force, he took a step backwards. His eyes narrowed.

'What do you know of my daughter?'

Bella curled her fingers round the gun in her coat pocket. It gave her confidence.

'Your daughter found out you took a white mistress even before your wife died, knew that when your whore died you visited her grave here every week, like a thief in the night. She thought she must have meant more to you than her own mother.'

Hussein's eyes bulged and his fists bunched. 'Who are you?' he rasped. 'How did you know my daughter and how dare you speak of such things to me?'

She ignored his questions and continued: 'She told me how you tried to force her into an arranged marriage while all the time you had sullied the sanctity of marriage, carrying on behind your dear wife's back. She knew what an old hypocrite you were. You drove your daughter away, Hussein, drove her to her death.'

Overcome with anger, he took a step towards her, his fist raised. She was ready for it and stepped back, pulling the gun from her pocket. When he saw the weapon, he halted and held up his hand like a shield.

'Thought you'd have guessed,' she said, 'or are you just being slow on the uptake like you were with your daughter.'

She watched as understanding penetrated to the core of his being, first intermingled with disbelief, then with growing certainty until it was set in stone. In shock, he stepped further back until his legs were pressed against the gravestone.

'You're his sister,' he said, his voice an angry whisper.

'And you're his murderer,' she came back at him venomously.

He managed to straighten up, conquer his emotions. 'I loved my daughter in spite of what you say, and your brother deserved everything he got. You were no better and your turn is coming, so do what you have to do while you still can.'

'Don't worry. I intend to. But I want to know where Macdonald is hiding. I've been to his home and he isn't there, so where is he?'

'Go to hell!'

'Not until I've sent all your family there. If you don't co-operate, they're dead.' She showed him her mobile in her free hand. 'I've people I can call on. They're watching your sons right now and one call is all it will take.'

Hussein hesitated, then hung his head and said, 'I don't know where he is. He contacts me through an old army pal named Eddie. That's all I know, so get on with it and leave my family alone.'

She thought about what he'd told her. She knew about Eddie, figured it made sense and it was all she was going to get out of Hussein who probably didn't give a damn about the doc so didn't need to lie. The bit about killing his family had been all bluff anyway, and she didn't want to linger too long here, risk being disturbed.

She looked up at the sky and whispered. 'This is for you, brother.' Then she pulled the trigger three times in quick succession.

Hussein clutched his stomach, tottered backwards, spun round, sprawled over the gravestone, his arms embracing the cold stone.

'Go and join your whore,' Bella said as she turned and hurried away. Half her duty to her brother had been completed.

CHAPTER 32

She'd already watched Macdonald's house for two days before deciding Alex wasn't around. That was when she'd decided to take out Hussein, try to find out what he knew of the doc's whereabouts. After killing Hussein she returned to the house, hid the car in the same barn her brother had used when he'd escaped. She still had the keys Alex had given her so she let herself in.

Eddie, according to what Hussein had told her before he died, seemed to be the key to finding Macdonald. She searched for the doctor's telephone or address book, figuring it would contain Eddie's address. But it proved hard to find. After a fruitless search downstairs, she tried the upstairs bedrooms without success. She was sitting on a bed thinking where to look next when she heard a car approaching. Her hopes rose. Could this be Alex coming home to make everything easier for her?

Gun in hand, hidden behind the bedroom curtains, she watched the taxi draw up outside. Her hopes were dashed when only the driver, not Alex, got out and walked towards the house. Those hopes revived when she recognized the dark, swarthy individual approaching. She'd seen photographs of him in army uniform with the doc and was sure it was Eddie. But what was he doing here?

The door opened and footsteps entered the house. Fortunately, Eddie didn't come upstairs. She crept on to the landing, listened, trying to decide how she was going to tackle him. Then, deciding diplomacy might help her glean more than an outright threat would, she put her gun back in her pocket and took off her blond wig. Assuming an air of confidence, she started down.

She found him sitting in the living room. When she entered he looked up, startled. She feigned equal surprise, reeling back, away from him.

'Who are you?' she said, deliberately widening her eyes. 'What are you doing in this house?'

He stood up, held up both hands in a conciliatory gesture. 'There's no need to be afraid. I'm Alex Macdonald's friend. I might ask you the same questions, of course.'

'You must be Eddie,' she sighed, momentarily closed her eyes, pretending relief. 'For a moment I thought I'd stumbled upon a burglar.'

She watched him scrutinize her as he waited for her to identify herself. Eventually, his gaze drifted to her red hair. A gleam of understanding came into his eyes.

'Gloria,' he announced. 'You must be Gloria. That red hair—'

'Can't get away with anything with this red hair, can I?' she said, shuffling her feet like a coy schoolgirl.

She could see from his sudden reserve, a hint of coldness even, that he knew the manner of her running away from his friend, was wondering now what possible reason she could have for returning to the house.

She fluttered her eyes coquettishly, hoping to distract him from those thoughts, make him think she was empty-headed and harmless.

'You'll think I'm awful,' she cried, 'leaving Alex the way I did. I was in such shock.'

From the set of his chin it was obvious that that tactic wasn't working.

'It all worked out,' he told her. 'He's back with his wife and daughter.'

'Oh! You think....'

'What?'

'You think I'm here to try to get back with him?'

'Aren't you?'

She pretended to be hurt. 'I'm far too ashamed of running away when he needed me most to even hope. I'm pleased it's worked out for him. I really am.'

She noticed him visibly relax, was sure she'd fooled him. But the remnants of suspicion were in the tone of his next question.

'So what are you doing here?'

'I still have my key. I came back for some things. I intended to leave Alex a note apologizing for my panicky exit.' She paused, asked him casually, 'Are you here for any particular reason, Eddie?'

He sighed. 'Alex's been in deep trouble and gone away for a while. I've been watching the house for him. He rings me here every other day.' He glanced at his watch. 'In fact he'll be calling any minute.'

The way he said it, she knew those last words were a hint that he wanted to be alone to take the call. But she had other ideas. Taking a handkerchief from her pocket, she dabbed at her eyes.

'You OK?' he asked gruffly.

She put the handkerchief away and leaned on the arm of the sofa as though she needed support.

'Do you think I could talk to him?'

Eddie looked doubtful. 'I don't think it would do either of you any good, to be frank. He's got a lot on his mind.'

She lowered her head. 'Please allow me to. I have a conscience, you see, and if I could just apologize to Alex for my behaviour, for letting him down, I would feel better. One word and then I'll go and leave you to your own business, I promise.'

She watched him trying to decide. In a curious way she admired his loyalty to his friend, his desire to protect him. Loyalty was one thing she understood. Fraternal loyalty was, after all, the reason she was here.

After a moment he looked straight at her, his eyes penetrating hers. 'You'll make it quick?'

Smiling inwardly, she nodded. 'Just an apology. It would mean so much.'

'Very well. But then you really will have to leave. We have some private matters to discuss.'

'Thank you, Eddie,' she said and slid on to the sofa.

The next few minutes seemed to drag. She hated small talk, sensed he did too. Silences stretched to embarrassment but she managed to say enough between them to keep it bearable, to stop him thinking too much, because she was afraid he might have second thoughts about letting her talk to Macdonald. Then the phone rang and Eddie picked it up. As he'd expected, it was Alex on the other end.

After preliminary greetings, Eddie said, 'This will be a surprise to you but I have Gloria with me. I found her in the house. She wants a quick word.'

She took that as her cue. Rising from the sofa, she stood next to Eddie. He stood up, handed the phone to her and said, 'He's surprised but agreeable.'

She sat down with the phone in the chair Eddie had vacated. He ambled over to the sofa.

She used her free hand to pull the gun from her pocket and pointed it at Eddie. His body jerked backwards as though hit by an electric shock. His eyes widened in amazement.

'What are you playing at?' he snapped.

He made to get out of the chair but froze halfway when he saw her tilt the weapon towards him and the grim way she was looking at him. Obviously she wasn't joking.

She waved the gun in his direction like a wand. A smile touched her lips but it didn't reach her eyes and there was real malice behind it, the smile of the assassin. Eddie realized it and sank back into the chair, nonplussed by the change in her.

'I'm not playing, Eddie! Listen and learn!'

She put the phone to her mouth and ear. She kept the gun pointing at Eddie when she spoke into the mouthpiece.

'It's time for reckoning, Alex. I've got my gun trained on your pal here. It'll be no trouble to kill him just like I did Hussein. You'll hear that on the news pretty soon, by the way, just in case you doubt my capabilities. And just so you know, my name is Bella not Gloria. You were living with Charles Bridge's sister. How does that grab you?'

From his chair, Eddie glared at her as the full extent of her machinations dawned on him. She, meanwhile, just listened to Alex's stuttering reply with a satisfied smile.

After a moment, she spoke again. 'That's right, Eddie's going to die. But you can save him. Meet me on the top of Danby Beacon sunrise tomorrow and he walks away free.'

With that, she put the phone down. She studied Eddie for his reaction. He was saying nothing but she could feel his hostility even across the room.

'It's going to be a long night and I can't trust you, Eddie. Going to have to lock you in the cellar and tie you up while I sleep.'

'He's no fool. He won't come,' Eddie told her, finding his voice.

'Oh, he'll come,' she replied. 'I know him well enough to know that. He won't let his old friend die and he'll believe he can get you away and still save himself.'

'He'll have the police with him,' Eddie said.

'That's why I chose to meet on Danby Beacon. He knows I'll be able to see everything for miles around. When he hears about

Hussein he'll know I'm quite prepared to kill you if he tries anything. I doubt he'll risk the police especially when he's been involved in plotting a prison escape himself.'

Eddie shook his head. 'How did he ever get entangled with you?'

She laughed. 'He was easy meat, alone and vulnerable. Not my type normally, but he served his purpose.'

'You inveigled your way into his life just so you could help your brother?'

'No wonder you only made sergeant in the army,' she snapped. 'The penny hasn't dropped, it's still falling.'

She made him go through to the kitchen, then down the wooden stairs to the cellar. There was enough rope there and she made him tie himself to the banister before stepping in herself to tighten the knots and make certain he was securely tied.

'Get some sleep, Sergeant,' was her parting shot. 'Reveille will be before sunset and we'll have a long climb to the top of the Beacon.'

Alex sat down at the kitchen table and stared into space, his face pained. He needed to tell Liz about the phone call from Gloria but found it hard to begin, to disappoint her again just when things seemed to be looking up. She'd been the one who'd persuaded him to put his conscience aside. Every time he tried to do that the demons returned with their accusations, as though nothing could subdue them for long. Now it was Eddie's turn to suffer because of him. Aside from that, there was the shock of finding that Gloria was Bridge's sister. That explained so much but it was humiliating to have to tell Liz how easily he'd been duped, to the extent of allowing a female viper in to his home. What had he been thinking? Was it all down to loneliness, or was some of it weakness of character and bad judgement?

Liz soon noticed that he was distracted. Fortunately Ann was out of the room so, raising a quizzical eyebrow, she tackled him head on.

'It's bad news, isn't it. Come on, man. Don't shut me out again.'

He took a deep breath and told her it all. When he had finished he put his elbows on the table, his head in his hands, and waited for her response.

She said nothing. He knew that, with her sanguine approach to life, she was trying to find an answer to the problem. But what room was there for optimism when there were lives at stake? His life or Eddie's. Take your pick.

'Whatever I do,' he groaned, 'I can't let her kill Eddie. He's my pal and he went the extra mile trying to help me.'

'You could call the police – anonymously. Let them tackle her. You could stay out of it. Give them only the bare bones so they can rescue Eddie.'

Alex lifted his head, looked straight at her. She couldn't meet his gaze, dropped her eyes.

'Sure I could ring the police and stay out of it. But what would that make me? He's my – our friend and he's taken big risks for us. I have to do my very best for him. You know that.'

'Maybe she's bluffing,' Liz said weakly, desperation in her voice.

'She's not bluffing, woman. She's already killed Hussein.'

Liz blanched at that cold fact. 'My God! What are we going to do?'

Alex sighed. 'I'm going to meet her on Danby Beacon. I'm sick of running away, Liz, and I won't run out on Eddie.'

One look at his face and she realized there was no arguing with him.

'I'll come with you,' she said, resigning herself to it.

Touched by her loyalty, however impractical, he managed a gentle smile.

'I don't think so. One of us has to be with Ann in case—'

'She succeeds in killing you. Because that's what will happen if you go.'

Alex took her hand. 'It's a possibility, I have to admit. But you know my feelings. Right now I'm going to rest in the bedroom, think this right through.'

Liz nodded her head, said sadly, 'How have things ever come to this?'

'Because I allowed them to,' he answered.

CHAPTER 33

The sun peeped over the horizon. Like luminous tentacles, its rays spilled over the long ribbon of dark sky, resurrecting the North Yorkshire moors in the triumph of light over darkness, giving fresh hope and impetus to all life.

Perched on a bare rock, more concerned with death and darkness than light, and without time or inclination for aesthetic appreciation, Bella watched that inexorable dawning. Close by, Eddie sat cross-legged in the bracken, his hands tied. He was exhausted, partly from the long tramp to the top of Danby Beacon but mainly from the debilitating effect of the drug Bella had given him, before they'd set out from Hope Farm, to dull his senses and therefore make him more easily manageable. She, on the other hand, felt a keen sense of exhilaration; the drug she had taken was to keep her going, give her a high. Right now, it made her feel she could conquer the world.

'No sign of police,' she muttered, using the binoculars around her neck to scan the roads which led to Danby Beacon. 'But there is a car parking up. Someone's getting out.'

She watched for some time until she was sure it was Alex Macdonald plodding up the long incline. Then she stood up and, with a satisfied smirk, held the binoculars to Eddie's eyes so he could see for himself.

'Told you he'd come,' she exclaimed. 'How noble the bastard

is. I could almost admire him for it, if he wasn't responsible for what happened to my poor Charles.'

Eddie listened to more of her ranting against his friend but said nothing. He felt too tired to respond. But it made no difference to Bella because, on a high, she was speaking mainly to herself, letting off her excess of steam as she anticipated the reckoning with her brother's nemesis in the form of the lonely figure climbing the hill.

She perched herself back on the rock, her red hair aflame as the sun burst on to the beacon.

'Not long now,' she murmured to herself, licking her lips like an alcoholic anticipating a longed for drink. 'Not long now, Charles, my darling.'

Dressed in a yellow parka, Alex stood out against the green and brown of the bracken. His hands were in plain view, no weapon in sight, when he halted thirty yards from them.

'Don't stop,' she yelled and bit down on her lip. She pointed at Eddie. 'Your pal's waiting for you.'

'Let him go,' Alex shouted back. 'Then I'll come the rest of the way.'

Bella hesitated for a moment. Then she grabbed Eddie and hauled him to his feet.

'Keep well away from him,' she shouted into Eddie's ear. 'Pass within ten yards and I'll shoot you. Believe me, I'm a good enough shot to take you both down.'

Wearily, Eddie started down the slope, his movement slow and clumsy. When he was level with Alex, there were fifteen yards between them.

'Don't worry about this, old son,' Alex shouted across to him. 'None of it's your fault. Just watch over Liz and Ann for me.'

Eddie stood still for a moment. Like a drunk, he stared bleary-eyed at Alex, then took a step towards him. Alex held up a hand.

'Keep going down that hill,' he shouted in his best sergeant-major voice, then, in a gentler tone. 'Believe me, I'm ready for this.'

His command penetrated the foggy patches in his friend's brain, which were making him sluggish. Eddie responded by looking up the hill at Bella who was watching them, her arm outstretched and her gun pointing in their direction. Then, hunching his shoulders as though all the troubles in the world were balanced there, he trudged off down the hill.

'Thought he would never go,' Bella chirped as Alex began the final part of his ascent. 'Has he no romance in his soul? Hasn't he heard of a lover's tryst? Doesn't he know we have to be alone one more time?'

Alex halted five yards from her. He could tell she was high. 'Didn't know you were a drug addict,' he stated, his voice matter-of-fact.

'Only on special occasions,' she came back at him. 'Like funerals, for instance, though having to live with you nearly drove me to it.'

He shook his head. 'Have to admit you were good. Had me fooled all along. You were wasted on crime. Should have been an actress.'

'You were easy meat, darling. Not my type, but what is it they say? A kiss is just a kiss. You can wipe it off afterwards, can't you? What you can't replace is a brother.'

'Do you think I'm that same fool you and your brother took me for?' There was a hint of menace in Alex's voice as he stared at the gun which was trained on him.

His body language and lack of fear threw her. She glowered at him.

'Only a fool would have tried it on with my brother. Only a fool would have walked up here knowing what was waiting for him.'

'Your brother? What was he? Just another criminal eating

away at other people's lives. A parasite on humanity's backside. He deserved what he got.'

Bella's face flushed. He'd pushed all her buttons and her trigger finger started to flex.

'Hold it right there!'

The parade ground authority in his command surprised her, caused her to pause. She'd been expecting him to plead for his life, but so far there'd been no sign of weakness. Cool as you like, he was even giving her an order. It wasn't good enough. Before she dispatched him to eternity, he needed to suffer as her brother had. She wanted the satisfaction of watching him perched on the cusp of oblivion, regretting what had brought him there. Seizing on her hesitation, he spoke up again.

'You'd better make it a killing shot because there's a police sniper on either side of your position and I'm not going to stand still.'

Her eyes flickered both ways. There was nothing but heather and gorse. She watched Alex warily, figuring that he was bluffing, that this was a last-ditch attempt to distract her, to give him an opportunity to rush her. He had some nerve. She'd give him that.

'You're the one on drugs,' she opined, her confidence returning.

Alex smiled, slowly lifted his hand in the air. As though fashioned from the earth itself two figures emerged from the ground, positioned exactly as he'd indicated. They were covered head to toe in grass and bracken and their faces were blacked. Each had instantly assumed a marksman's stance, weapons pointing at Bella. Intense concentration and their silence only added to their other-worldly, devilish aura.

There was a mad look in Bella's eyes. She understood now her adversary's coolness. She hadn't expected him to involve the police because he would be incarcerated himself for his part in her brother's escape. Of course, she'd expected he might try something but, having taken him for a fool on previous form, nothing she wouldn't be able to handle. Yet, what did it matter in the end? He was still exactly where she wanted him.

'Big miscalculation,' Alex said, watching her gun. 'You see I'd rather go to prison than lose my life. Pretty obvious trade-off, really.'

She laughed. 'But you came, didn't you? That's all I needed.'

Alex frowned. Bella had a maniacal look in her eye. This wasn't going to end as easily as he'd hoped. Whether because of the drugs, or infatuation with her brother, she didn't look as though she was going to be diverted from her purpose.

'Put the gun down,' he said. 'You haven't a chance. He isn't worth dying for.'

Bella pursed her lips. 'It was you who miscalculated. I'm not bothered about living or dying with my brother gone. Prison certainly has no appeal. At least I'll have the satisfaction of taking you with me.'

Alex saw the gun start to come up. 'Don't!' he yelled his heart pounding against his chest as though it was about to burst its confines.

'See you in hell!' she screeched.

Alex dived to one side. Two loud reports echoed in his ears. Anticipation of the bullet which would end his life as well as a myriad thoughts of Liz and Ann were compressed into the unforgiving seconds before he hit the ground.

The bracken cushioned his fall but the jolt stunned him. Instinct made him roll on to his back, surprised that he couldn't feel any pain. He looked up, was conscious of a shadowy figure hovering over him, blotting out the sun. As his focus grew sharper he saw its arms were spread like angel's wings, as though they were about to gather him up and smother him in their embrace. Illuminated by the sun's rays, the head was an incandescent, red halo. Fear clutched at him. Was he dying after all and at the mercy of a supernatural being?

Clarity soon followed bemusement. This was no angel; it was Bella. She unbalanced and he tried to roll but she landed on top of him. Her face was next to his, wide eyes fixed on him as though she would never let him out of her sight. Intermingled blood and grey matter poured out of her head from a bullet wound. Disgusted, he pushed her dead body off and staggered to his feet.

The police marksmen had closed in. They stood at a respectful distance while he was sick.

'Will you be OK?' one of them asked.

Half-bending over, wiping his mouth, Alex cocked his head to look at them. 'Thanks to you I will.'

'Sorry it came to this,' the other one said. 'It was a close thing and she gave us no choice.'

'Don't let it bother you,' Alex told them, straightening and brushing grey brain matter off his clothes. 'She knew what she was doing. She wanted to die and if it hadn't been for your expertise I'd be with her.'

A radio crackled and one of the men spoke into his mouth-piece. Alex, with one last glance at Bella's prone body, started down the hill.

Eddie was asleep in the back of the car, snoring. Whatever Bella had given him must have drained him, the effort of coming down the hill depleting his last reserves of energy. Alex, tired himself, leaned against the car and didn't wake him. He felt a shiver run through his body. As a soldier and doctor he'd seen some grotesque sights, but Bella's death had shocked him. Her death, any death at such a young age, seemed such a waste, the antithesis of his own aspirations as a doctor. He sighed with the weight of his melancholia. Never could he have anticipated any of this when he'd set out in his new profession. He'd been full of ideals then but they'd come to nothing in the end.

Minutes later an unmarked police car drove up the single track and parked. DI Johnson got out of the passenger side. He strode towards Alex and glanced at Eddie in the back seat.

'She's given him a drug,' Alex told him. 'He'll need an ambulance.'

'One on its way,' Johnson said, assessing Alex's own condition with his blue eyes. 'How about yourself. Need any medical attention?'

'I'm still standing,' Alex grunted.

'Well, if it's any consolation, you did the right thing,' Johnson told him.

Alex looked back up the hill, squeezed his eyes shut.

'Why the hell did she have to do it? He wasn't worth it.'

'Twisted sense of loyalty,' Johnson surmised, 'or some psychological need. Who knows? We're all different, aren't we? There's shades of black and white in all of us. It's a delicate balance, easily upset.'

Alex gave him a quizzical look. Johnson hadn't seemed the type to set much store in psychological analysis.

'Think so?'

'Know so from experience. Take yourself. You're law-abiding, self-disciplined, but you made one slip when they found a weakness.' Johnson paused, allowed his eyes to drift over the moors with their ever-changing landscape. 'Some might say you were justified, even. But in the eyes of the law it was a wrong action and we all need the law, don't we?'

Alex looked glum. 'Whatever, I'll go to prison for it, and in one way it'll be a relief to pay my dues.'

'You probably will go to prison,' Johnson said, his tone sombre. 'But what you did today will help you. When the court knows the pressure you were under, the fact that woman was even living with you, I think they'll be very lenient.'

'How long do you think?'

Johnson drew in a breath, pondered the question. 'Nothing is certain but with time off for good behaviour, I'd say a year, maybe two if you're unlucky. Don't take that as gospel though.'

'I think I can manage that,' Alex said, 'as long as Liz and Ann support me.'

Johnson squeezed Alex's shoulder with his big hand. 'I've already talked to them. No worries there. They're solid.'

An ambulance drove up at full speed. Two paramedics got out. Johnson pointed to Eddie. They hauled him gently out of the car and on to a stretcher. He was still asleep when they carried him past Alex and the policeman.

'He must be a good friend,' Johnson stated.

'The best. We go a long way back.'

Johnson scratched his nose. 'Don't suppose he aided and abetted?'

'Innocent bystander,' Alex said, deadpan.

'Ready?' the policeman asked.

Alex managed a wistful smile. 'Yes, I'm ready to be fed to the lions.'

Alex sat in the back of the car beside Johnson. As it drove away, he glanced up at the Beacon, vowed one day, in a new life, he'd come back here with Liz and Ann. Love, their love, was all that mattered, all that could endure in this crazy life where the winds of fate did not always blow gently. He'd lost that perspective for a while but he had it back now. When he'd paid his dues, he'd make it up to them. By God, would he!